Summer Children

Summer Children

Ready or Not For School

by
James K. Uphoff June E. Gilmore
Rosemarie Huber
Illustrations by Jacque L. Cross

Printed by The Oxford Press
3rd Printing

ISBN-0-9618561-0-6

We dedicate this book to our spouses, children and grandchildren and to all those summer children - born and unborn - who may benefit from our research and this book.

JU, JG, RH, JC

Introduction

This book was just meant to be written.

We have no doubt about that; nor about the fact that the four of us (June, Jim, Jacque and I) were destined to meet and work together. For our working union, you see, was like many of those strange, "meant to be" situations in life - the result of coincidence and a criss-crossing, overlapping network of activities and interests.

The starting point, I suppose, was in spring of 1983 when June (a psychologist in the Cincinnati Public School System) decided to run for the presidency of the Ohio School Psychologists group. As part of her candidacy for that office, she had listed an unpublished study on **summer children** and the effects of enrolling a child in school too early.

Upon seeing that reference, a colleague from another area of the state wrote to June and requested a copy of the study. "When I called to tell her that it wasn't actually written up yet," June explains, "she said she had seen a newspaper article referencing a similar study by a professor at Wright State University in Dayton (Ohio)."

Enter - you guessed it - Dr. James Uphoff. It seems that in the spring of 1980 while checking over the thesis of one of his graduate students, he had a rather memorable experience. "As I read her paper, which dealt with **summer children** and early school entrance," he recalls, "I felt as if it were a mirror reference of someone I know quite well - me!"

In that rather cursory grad student treatment of the academic, social and emotional effects of **too much, too soon** for some children, Jim could reflect back and vividly recall similar handicaps and problems that he had experienced as a **summer** child and as one of the youngest in his class. The subject so intrigued him that he was motivated to take a sabbatical in the spring of 1982 to pursue and expand the data. Which he did.

Back to June. Upon learning about Jim's work, she wasted no time in tracking him down; and the two met in Dayton to compare notes and data. To their academic delight they found that even though their studies had taken place at different times and in different parts of the country, their figures and findings overlapped and supported their mutual theory.

A book was inevitable. Enter - me.

About the time all this was going on (we're up to August of 1983 now), I was working on a full-page newspaper feature (I'm a free lance writer) on one of my favorite pet peeves - pushing youngsters into too much, too soon. As the mother of four young boys who found the pressures of T-ball, D-ball, soccer, Scouts, music lessons, etc., (not to mention that minor responsibility of school) to be taxing not only for me, but also for the boys, I (along with my husband) made a conscious decision to be selective and limited in helping our boys choose extracurricular activities.

I also wanted to write about this; but, of course, I needed some professional backup on the article. So I scoured up the head of the children's department at the local library, a pre-school teacher and a male child psychologist. To round out the interview, I thought it would be good to get the viewpoint of a female child psychologist. So I opened the Yellow Pages and called the first listing I found - that of June Gilmore.

If June had not been pleased with that feature story, I probably wouldn't be writing this. But she was; so she called to ask if I might be interested in a rather expansive, joint writing project; and we were on our way.

Once we had our outline together, the need for an artist became apparent. Enter - Jacque Cross. "Jac" and June go back a long way to the days when they were quite involved with special education and the Council for Exceptional Children. Jacque was, in fact, a director in the Division of Special Education, Ohio Department of Education; and June, an intern school psychologist.

That's basically how the four of us became the academic "parents" of all the **summer children** described and illustrated in this volume.

Like any parents, we're proud of these "summer kids" of ours - from "Monday's Child" who is "fair of face," through "Thursday's Child" who "has far to go" and up to and including "Sunday's Child" who is "fair and wise and good."

We hope that you enjoy reading about these youngsters and about their situations. More importantly, however, we hope that the findings contained in the studies presented help you to make positive and helpful decisions about the most important **summer children** in the world - YOURS!

Rosemarie Huber
June 1986

TABLE OF CONTENTS

Forward

Monday's child is fair of face,

Tuesday's child is full of grace,

Wednesday's child is full of woe,

Thursday's child has far to go,

Friday's child is loving and giving,

Saturday's child works hard for a living,

And the child that's born on the Sabbath Day,

is fair and wise and good and gay."

-Mother Goose

Here I come! Ready or N-O-O-O-T!!!"

A popular cry from the generations-old "hide and seek" game, this favorite chant can be heard over and over from Monday's Child, Tuesday's Child - yes, from just about everyone who is or who has ever been young.

Perhaps "hide and seek" has remained a favorite recreation of youngsters because just about everyone starts out on an even footing. Even Wednesday's Child (who might occasionally appear "full of woe") stands a chance to be a "winner."

In the more challenging game of life, however, things are a lot different. For in real life, it is Sunday's Child who seemingly has the upper edge at success. Ah, WOULD that all children COULD be born on the Sabbath Day. How wonderful it would be to have a

1

generation of youngsters, all "fair and wise and good. . ." And how unutterably boring.

While most parents and educators WOULD not opt for such childhood perfection (even if they COULD), those same adults who, day in and day out, deal with children will be the first to bemoan the frustrations, aggravations and disappointments that naturally occur in the education and upbringing of youngsters. You're probably one of those adults. Now, don't deny it. Being a parent or teacher has countless and endless rewards. But, by golly, you have to have the patience of Job, the constitution of Hercules and the sense of humor of Bill Cosby to endure some days.

Our parents probably thought the same thing. Plus, they were raising kids without the help of microwave ovens. And we think we have it tough! Truth is, we DO have it tough - in some cases, tougher than parents of other generations and eras.

True, today we do not have to cope with huge epidemics of plague, polio and other childhood diseases which, thanks to medical science, have been all but obliterated. We do not have to spend 90% of our time on domestic chores, again thanks to all the marvelous, new time-saving inventions which have been introduced in the years since World War II. And, in many cases, we do not even have to shoulder the challenges of child-rearing COMPLETELY alone, what with the help of day-care centers and nursery schools for working parents, of support groups for every doubt, fear and neurosis you can think of and of skads and skads of TV and radio programs, lecture series and books (like this one) which claim they will help you do the job.

And we all need help because we all live under the strain of tremendous pressures - pressures which know no age limits. Unfortunately, our kids are not spared this hectic, lightening- fast, 1980s way of life. They, too, experience pressures that would never have crossed a youngster's mind in previous generations. Ironically enough, it is that same stepped-up technology that brought us the Salk polio vaccine, color TV sets and the phenomenal computer that is also responsible for some of the modern pressures and strains that are inflicted on youngsters as young as three years old.

We can blame Sputnik, in part, for the trend. When the Soviet Union launched their satellite in 1957, the United States reacted with concern that American schools were not keeping up with the Russians. Consequently, there was a major "push down" effort in curriculums across the country. What had been a typical first-grade curriculum began to show up in kindergarten. The "play" stuff of kindergarten crawled down into the pre-schools. And five-year-olds who used to color, learn to skip and hang from monkey bars during their first exposure to formal education were also attempting to master the beginnings of phonics and letter sounds - skills that, at one time, were reserved for first and second graders.

No, we don't have to worry too much about polio anymore. But we are dealing today with a much more intangible and delicate problem - the growing pressures forced upon our youngsters at too early an age. If you question the validity of this concern, just ask yourself the following questions:

*Why would such noted magazines as *TIME* and *NEWSWEEK* devote cover stories and extensive features to the subject of forcing too much too soon upon too many youngsters?

*Why would such distinguished groups as the American Society of Pediatrics and the American Red Cross address themselves to the growing concern of stress symptoms in children?

*Why has the rate of teen-age suicide continued to rise at such a frightening pace?

*Why has an increasingly and alarmingly large number of youngsters been diagnosed as "learning disabled" in recent years?

*Why have standardized test scores declined so dramatically? "Why can't Johnny read?"

*Why do children who are, chronologically, the youngest in their classes experience failure at a much greater rate than their older peers - even though the younger children, in many instances, have higher IQs?

*Why is a group in Ohio working to change the cutoff date for the age-five entrance requirement into kindergarten from September 30 to June 30?

*Why has a group of Racine, Wisconsin parents banded together to form Children Need Childhood, an

3

organization claiming that youngsters are being asked to learn too much too soon?

Or, closer to home, you may be asking yourself questions about your own child or those who are your students. Why, for instance, does a child with an above-average IQ produce sub-standard work in the classroom?

Why does your neighbor's kindergarten youngster feel comfortable with such class projects as painting and cutting while your own 5-year-old begins every task with the cry, "I can't do it" - even though he can?

Why does one child barely whisper when she's called on in class while another is incessantly noisy and disruptive?

Or take this parent/teacher test: How many times have you found yourself saying or thinking, "He COULD do better if he WOULD. . .

. . . only try

. . . try harder

. . . stop fooling around

. . . pay attention

. . . only concentrate

. . . not daydream

. . . blah, blah, blah, blah, blah, blah. . .

And that's about how it sounds to a young student who is frustrated with school - "blah, blah, blah, blah, blah" - gibberish! That's because there are thousands of kids today in elementary, middle and secondary schools across the country who are spinning their wheels when it comes to their education. They THINK they are paying attention, trying, concentrating, etc. They THINK they are working hard.

In truth, many of them are probably doing the best they can. It's not a matter of they COULD achieve if only they WOULD do such and such. It's more, they WOULD perform better if only they COULD. The first situation (They COULD achieve if only they WOULD . . .)

implies an attitudinal problem in that the child lacks the desire and/or motivation to perform. In the second situation, however, we have a child who might very likely have the desire to do better; but because of a lack of readiness, he or she is simply not able to do so.

The bottom line on all this is no big secret. What we're dealing with here is the question of physical, social and emotional readiness for school. Common sense tells us that not all five-year-olds are ready for entrance into a formal educational structure. Many parents through the years have recognized this fact and held their child back until he was more mature. This is particularly true in the case of little boys who have been found to lag behind their female peers at that age.

This does not imply that girls do not benefit from a delayed entrance into school. Quite the contrary. It has been found, in fact, that girls actually benefit more by the delayed start.

There have been countless articles written on the subject, numerous debates on the appropriate cutoff date for kindergarten entrance. Some have even posed the question of whether or not the mandatory age five for starting school has outlived its usefulness.

But not until our study has any researcher produced concrete statistics that show that **summer children,** those children born between approximately June 1st and December 31st and who start school in the year they first become eligible, are more fit for academic failure. (NOTE: Dates are arbitrary. Many youngsters with birthdays prior to June 1st and after December 31st could certainly fall within this category.) In addition, our studies show that these same youngsters experience more social and emotional problems than their counterparts who are held back a year before beginning kindergarten.

In another pilot study which we are presently undertaking, the alarming trend seems to indicate that this same group of **summer children** who were placed in school before age five years, six months, are more prone to suicide in their teen-age and young adult years.

While our numbers verified what we had suspected all along, we figured that our findings would be met with the greatest scepticism from our colleagues in the Ohio School Psychologists Association. To our surprise and delight, however, when we presented the results of our studies at the 1984 Annual Conference in May of that year, not one professional challenged our thesis. Not one psychologist grilled us on the validity of our conclusions.

Rather, our attention-getting premise that anyone under the age of five years, six months has no business in a formal classroom situation, was met with agreeably nodding heads, with comments like, "Yes, this is just what we've observed, but we had no data to back up our theory." Or, "We've had a gut feeling all along that this was true."

We feel so strongly, in fact, about our premise that we are willing to stick our necks out on the chopping block and issue a **CAUTION** statement:

We feel, on the basis of research we have done and after reviewing data provided by others, that we are tempted to say that EVERY child under the age of five years, six months should wait a year before starting kindergarten.

While many parents will argue the "exceptional" quality of their child, we feel that even though a youngster may be academically talented, he is still not physically, socially and emotionally mature enough to do justice to the experience of formal education as it exists today. Those few children who might be exceptions are so rare that they would be immediately spotted in a kindergarten screening and appropriate adjustments would be made. Truly gifted children are a separate concern.

It must be emphasized that being bright and being developmentally ready are two entirely different things. We realize, of course, that there will always be an older and a younger element in the classroom. Beyond pure age considerations, we are interested in a broader goal - to have all children in any given classroom developmentally ready so that each child in the class can learn more easily and more rapidly. When this goal has been successfully met, then the entire group of youngsters can progress at a faster pace.

We feel so strongly, in fact, about our goal and about the value of the findings of our research and the value of our **CAUTION** statement that we are writing this book to elaborate on the subject. In the following pages you will find more detailed explanations of the problems of **summer children**, including the findings and comments of many other authorities. Possible answers and hopefully helpful suggestions to deal with your own child are also included.

Our main concern here is the **summer child,** the child who is pushed ahead too quickly, snowed under with too much, too soon, the child who WOULD if only. . . he COULD!

Monday's Child

"Fair of Face"

"Fair of Face"

Just as beauty is only skin deep, total success is much more than just IQ deep. Unfortunately, someone forgot to tell this to many of today's parents, particularly a good number of post- War baby-boomers who are belatedly becoming parents themselves. It seems that this particular group (who, ironically enough, are the same kids who were victims of the late 1950s Sputnik hype and push for education) is changing the course of childhood. You might even say they are taking the "child" out of childhood, replacing him with a miniature adult form who is made to feel inferior if he cannot read before entering kindergarten.

When this sort of thing happens, that fair face of childhood may be sadly transformed from one glowing with sparkling eyes and innocent smiles to a countenance which appears old for its years.

Educators who are beginning to pick up on the frustrations of modern-day childhood are discussing in their faculty meetings such issues as childhood stress. And it's not at all unusual to pick up publications or to tune into media coverage on the subject.

More than one modern-day parent has expressed outrage because his preschooler has "graduated" from two years of classes and still cannot read, for heaven's sake! "Kindergarten is too late!" they protest - these baby-boomer parents who are older, more educated, more affluent than mothers and fathers of past generations. They have lived through competition and they know it's fierce. They have to push their children toward a goal; and they have to start early.

And so you have parents who will shell out $2000 a year to see that baby gets into a highly academic preschool and "learns to read" by the age of three. You have mothers who cry when told their child is of "average" intelligence. You have fathers who will fight to get their kid enrolled in kindergarten, even though the youngster doesn't quite make the cutoff date for entrance.

In short, this generation of parents has turned the ABC's of

10

child-rearing upside down. In a cover story on "Bringing Up Superbaby," *Newsweek* magazine referred to the ABCs of the 1980s as **Anxiety, Betterment, Competition.** Pediatrician T. Berry Brazelton of Harvard even laments, "Everyone wants to raise the smartest kid in America rather than the best adjusted, happiest one."

In a love-blind motivation to help their children learn more and to learn earlier than ever, many of today's parents are innocently turning their fair-faced youngsters into little people whose wide-eyed childhood characteristics might actually be masking inner anxieties and stress. It is such an atmosphere that has led some experts, in a complete turn-around from the thinking of the late fifties, to say that too much education too soon can possibly backfire!

"I worry that these kids will be overintellectualized," says none other than the respected Dr. Benjamin Spock, the pediatric guru by whose precepts so many of today's parents were raised. "Being persuaded that the most important thing is to be bright and get good grades may move people away from the natural, emotional ways of dealing with life," he warns.

Psychologist Lee Salk carries this mode of thought one step further. "This pressure for high achievement really sets children up for failure," he believes.

Intense early learning, in fact, is drawing fire from many psychologists because it may impede other skills necessary for total growth and maturity in childhood. "Pressure for academic achievement can take away something from other agendas, such as the development of social skills," according to Craig Ramey of the University of North Carolina.

It's not at all unusual to pick up a newspaper or magazine and read headlines such as: **Accelerated Learning Harmful, Educator Says.** In just the same way, it's not at all unusual for a parent to read such a headline and think, "But MY child is different."

It is precisely this type of thinking that has led to kindergarten classrooms filled with youngsters who are simply not ready for the tensions and rigors of formal education as it exists today in this country. Dr. Gwendolyn Wooddell, an associate professor at Wilmington College in Ohio (and once a kindergarten teacher herself) even goes so far as to say, "Speeding up reading instruction for children is one of the reasons Johnny can't read." In an address at the annual conference of the Midwest Association for the Education

11

of Young Children in May of 1984, Dr. Wooddell used a down-home illustration to prove her point. "If you bake a cake too fast, it doesn't come out right," she said, implying that the zeal that prompts some parents, school administrators and teachers to step up educational efforts can actually have a detrimental effect later on.

Before learning to read and write, children must develop certain skills - and they must develop them naturally. Dr. Wooddell, like many other professionals, is concerned that many youngsters are being taught to "read" and/or to "write" in a way that is out of sync. "Development," she explains, "follows an orderly sequence. When we force things in the cognitive area to happen out of order, we're ruining the natural process." Speeding up this process, many experts agree, can actually harm children socially, emotionally and physically as well as intellectually. After all, a child's intellect can hold only so much. And even though many parents are working hard to raise state-of-the-art kids, five-year-olds can achieve no more than their brain was designed for.

You don't have to have a Ph.D. to realize that the rate of development varies with each child. Children who walk and talk at an early age are not necessarily smarter than their slower counterparts. By the same token, Dr. Wooddell points out, "Slower doesn't mean dumber and physically inferior." That's why it seems almost ludicrous to assume that any child who has reached age five by August 30th, for instance, is physically, emotionally and socially prepared to enter kindergarten. It may seem just as ridiculous to say, as we are positing, that no child should enter the formal structure of kindergarten until he is five years, six months old. While we certainly admit to exceptions to this and just about anything else in education, we still stick to our **CAUTION** statement:

We feel, on the basis of research we have done and after reviewing data provided by others, that we are tempted to say that EVERY child under the age of five years, six months should wait a year before starting kindergarten.

Before we discuss how the fairness of childhood's face can fade in the light of academic failure, we'll provide a little information concerning how all this came about. Much research over the years has documented the fact that most school failure is experienced by a small portion of the school population -- the younger children in each class. The early data show this problem to be a sexist one, most likely to hit boys; but our later findings indicate that girls also have significant problems from too early an entrance into formal schooling.

Think about it. Take the youngsters whose birthdays fall at the beginning of March. When they turn five (the typical age of entrance into kindergarten), it will be the middle of an academic year. So they will actually be five years, six months old when they get around to starting school the following fall. A classmate born in August, on the other hand, will barely make the cutoff by the first of September. Obviously, fall-born children who are eligible to start school in their state will be even younger.

Common sense tells us that an additional six or more months of maturity, of life experiences and of mere physical growth can (at that tender age) make a world of difference in the academic and social readines of the child. Being professionals, however, we were not content with what common sense dictates. Rather, we needed numbers, charts and proof to show us that we were right on track where our theory is concerned.

We won't bore you here with all the scientific trappings of the studies. If you do wish to view our tables, however, they are provided in an appendix to this volume. For our purposes, let's talk about the real life data of our research which, by the way, was conducted independently, without one another's knowledge and in two different parts of the country.

One aspect of the research (Uphoff, 1982) was carried out in a school district which serves the county seat of Hebron, Nebraska (population estimated at 1800) and some surrounding rural areas and small towns (population estimated at 800). Hebron is located in the south central part of the state about 90 miles southwest of Lincoln. The area is essentially rural in character, philosophy and values. It has a strong northern European, especially German, background with Lutheran churches being in the majority.

There is a distinct reason for the choice of such a community. Our study primarily addresses itself to the question: **Do summer children experience more or less academic failure than non-summer children, including Held Back Summer Children?**

For our purposes of discussion, **summer children** is defined as children born between June 1st and September 30th (Gilmore's study) or June 1st and October 15th (Uphoff's study). **Held back**

summer children are those **summer children** whose entrance into kindergarten was delayed one year. The held back **summer children** are the "waiters."

It stands to reason that the environment where these problems would be **LEAST** likely to occur would be characterized by family stability, school stability and the likelihood of many adults knowing and having an impact on a child's life. The more adults who know a child and his/her family, the better chance this child will have in overcoming and/or preventing the potential problems of being among the youngest in the class.

The Hebron area was chosen as, more or less, an acid test for the theory. "I figured that if the youngest children in such a stable community are found to experience significant problems, then it would seem even more likely that children in typical urban and suburban environments would encounter these problems in even greater numbers and to greater degrees." (Uphoff, 1982).

This part of our research included all 278 pupils in grades K through six-students who came from stable, non-mobile, extended -family-available homes and who consistently scored above national norms on standardized tests. **Summer children** who started school in the year when they first became eligible numbered 63 or 22.67% of the total enrollment in the study. Held Back Summer children numbered 26 or 9.35% of the total.

From March 22nd through April 23rd 1982, and again in the summers of 1982, 1983 and 1984, much time was spent with these youngsters, with their school records, with the parents and with their teachers and counselors.

Meanwhile in another part of the country (unbeknownst to any one of us) the other aspect of what eventually was to become our joint research was going on. "I started screening potential kindergarten children for Cincinnati area parochial schools where, ironically enough, many children had late summer birthdays. Because holding these youngsters back a year would jeopardize the school's kindergarten program for the coming year, pushing them ahead seemed the thing to do." (Gilmore, 1983).

`"But I could not, in all good conscience, do that without answering a few questions for myself. I felt it essential to return to the Wapakoneta (Ohio) area to check on the progress of students whom I had screened seven years earlier when I was the school psychologist for the Wapakoneta City Schools. During my stint in that capacity I had conferred with the parents of the children I had screened for kindergarten, consistently recommending to the parents of **summer children** that they delay the start of their youngster's formal school experience for a year.

"Over a two-year period I had conferred with 500-600 parents of the children screened before entering school. Realizing that parents tend to over-estimate the significance of student scores on the kindergarten screening tests, I would recommend holding back the **summer children** BEFORE sharing the screening results with those parents. Thus all of the parents (even those with children whose scores indicated they should do well academically) were aware of the potential for problems."

Like the Hebron, Nebraska of Uphoff's study, Wapakoneta (aside from being well-known as the hometown of the first man on the moon, Neil Armstrong) is a relatively quiet, stable community whose students also consistently score above national norms in standardized testing.

"I returned to Wapakoneta in 1983 to gather data on the success of the students I had screened seven years before. Seventy of those **summer children** were still enrolled in the school system; and although not a part of any formal research design, 35 had been held back by their parents while 35 had started school when first eligible. The oldest of these 70 had completed sixth grade and the youngest had finished third grade when I collected my data from school records. This material, then, represented from four to seven years of information." (Gilmore, 1983).

Like Dr. Uphoff, "I soon discovered a significant pattern to the achievement levels of the **summer children** and the held back **summer children** in my study. And although the numbers involved in my project are relatively small, I (again like Dr. Uphoff) have found it scientifically possible to draw several conclusions which could have far-reaching implications." (Gilmore, 1983).

But first let's take a look at some of those numbers. Actually, the statistics on academic failure are probably the clearest and most simple. "In the Nebraska study I checked on those Hebron students who had repeated one or more grades. The results were dramatic and clear-cut. **Summer children** accounted for 75% of all such repeaters; and (to add even more credibility to the theory) not one - not ONE! - held back **summer child** had failed. These figures

15

become even more significant when we consider that **summer children** made up only 22.67% of the school population. Clearly, then, the summer children failed far in excess of any reasonable probability expectation." (Uphoff).

The Ohio data paint a similar picture. **Summer children** in that part of the study included 15 males and 20 females; for the held back **summer children** the split was 26 males and 9 females. When the votes were in it became apparent that the theory was panning out. Only one held back summer child, a boy, had failed a grade, thus accounting for a mere 2.86% of those studied. But four **summer children** (three boys, one girl) had been retained, for a figure of 11.43%.

While we were, individually, pleased and excited about these preliminary results of our work, we both realized that further research was needed to give our studies depth. When we finally met in Dayton (Ohio) and compared data, our enthusiasm was sparked even more. For our observations and conclusions mutually gave credibility to "talk" and comments that have been a part of educational literature for years, but always in the form of either unsubstantiated or rather weakly substantiated theory. Early studies had found problems before the curriculum was pushed down. There were good studies; but just no follow up.

Actually, as far back as 1952 (when those notorious baby- boomers were just starting to establish themselves in school) an article appeared in *The Elementary School Journal*. Written by Arthur E. Hamalainen, it addressed itself to "Kindergarten - Primary Entrance Age in Relation to Later School Adjustment." Incredible as it may seem, the article refers to a state where the desirable September age for a child entering kindergarten was 4 years, 9 months. In the 1949-50 study, 16.5% even fell below this cutoff but were still permitted to enroll in kindergarten.

Three years later, 33 principals were asked to state the most common problems they had observed with the underage (the ones who started kindergarten under the age of 4 years, 9 months), the normal age and the over-age children in their schools. The results showed that the scholastic difficulties of the youngest children were not confined to the first year of formal schooling alone. For 82% of the principals said that the underage children in grades one through three commonly faced problems in scholastic achievement.

A few years later in 1955 another article appeared in the same journal, this one by Inez B. King. Entitled "The Effect of Age of Entrance into Grade One Upon Achievement in Elementary School Adjustment," it, too, indicated that the younger students in a classroom (the summer children) were being set up for potential academic failure.

The study that King cites was conducted in Oak Ridge, Tennessee in 1946, a time when pupils were required to be six years old by (if you can believe this) December 31st in order to enter first grade. (Although many states have changed, some still have December 31st as a cutoff date.) Kindergarten at that time was available but not required. The study compared those youngsters who started before age six with those who were already six at the start of the school year. Group One included 54 children who were between the ages of five years, eight months and five years, 11 months at the start of the study. Group Two was comprised of 50 students between the ages of six years, five months and six years, eight months at the beginning of the first grade year. ALL the children followed had IQs of between 90 and 110, i.e., typical or average.

Just as we have concluded from our contemporary research, King deduced a disadvantage for the **summer child** from this study of the late 1940s:

"This study would seem to indicate that having attained a few additional months of chronological age at the beginning of grade one is an important factor in a child's ability to meet imposed restrictions and tensions that the school necessarily presents. With a group of children such as those included in this study, it appears likely that one can expect the following: Younger entrants will have difficulty attaining up to grade-level in academic skills, and a large portion of them may fall far below grade level-standards. Older entrants are more likely to achieve up to and beyond grade-level standards."

King further predicts that a large number of the younger entrants will have to repeat a grade; and that more boys than girls will repeat a grade. Sound familiar? It certainly does to us. But we're not the only ones who can tune into such a prediction.

More currently, the June, 1984, issue of *Better Homes and Gardens* also deals with the topic of academic failure. "Most retentions," the article by Dan Kaercher states, "occur in the lower

17

elementary grades, particularly in kindergarten and first grade. Even before kindergarten, a youngster's parents may be encouraged to have him wait an extra year before starting school. Educators agree that repeating a grade can do the most good and is least awkward early in the school career. It's also the time when parents have the most say about holding a youngster back."

Yes, it is the time when parents can have a say in the educational future of their child, when they can actually help program their **summer children** to either be fit for failure or set for success. Again, we reiterate our **Caution** statement:

We feel, on the basis of research we have done and after reviewing data provided by others, that we are tempted to say that EVERY child under the age of five years, six months should wait a year before starting kindergarten.

Unfortunately, this was not the thinking of the masses in the late 1950's. The studies we have previously cited are rare for that time period. For in the Sputnik era, the implied goal was to push children, not to hold back. This is the case in a study cited in the February, 1957 issue of *The Elementary School Journal.* In the article entitled, "Academic Achievement and Social Adjustment of Children Young for their Grade Placement," Vera V. Miller presented an accurate rundown of the thinking of the time.

She reported that a survey of 50 school systems in the Evanston, Illinois area revealed school entrance cutoff dates to be either November 30th or December 31st. To pacify teachers and parents who wanted their "bright" youngsters to get an early start, however, 12% of these districts had early admission procedure for those who were beyond the cutoff date. What's even more shocking (and detrimental as we view it today) is that 54% of those districts also used a "double promotion" system of pushing those youngsters through the grade levels when it seemed appropriate.

In all fairness, we must report here the results of that late fifties research - even though it is clearly contrary to what we have found to be true. Miller says in her article, "Careful analysis of the results indicated that these children (children young for their grade placement), on the whole, were well adjusted socially. . .The

18

achievement tests of these children revealed that, with rare exceptions, they were above average in academic achievement according to teacher judgment. They were above average in intelligence as indicated by mental test results. The data give little foundation for the concern that children younger than the average are injured by early admission to school."

In respect to these findings, we still must ask a few questions. Could it be that these children got through because of that higher than average intelligence level? Would the child of average intelligence have been as successful? We also question the quality level of the above average, younger students. While they faired well from a report standpoint, were they really achieving to their potential? Or were they, perhaps, underachieving?

It's interesting to note, however, that although this Illinois study just mentioned points to the conclusion that chronological age is not so important in the academic, social and emotional adjustment of children as many people think, Miller includes a statement that we find most significant:

"The child whose birthday comes in November or December is admitted without individual testing in a large percent of school districts reporting on the questionnaire. A larger percent of retentions and immaturities of various sorts are likely to be found here than in the younger age group admitted by test since these children represent a wide range of abilitities. It is sometimes suggested that an earlier cutoff point with testing required before admission of these youngsters would be more likely to result in successful adjustment in the primary grades."

This type of caution is certainly in line with our own philosophies and that of many contemporary experts. While we are dealing in this chapter primarily with academic failure, Dr. Grace Diamond, in a 1983 article in *The Journal of Learning Disabilities*, carried the plight of **summer children** one step further.

"As hypothesized," she says, "there is a significant correlation of percentage of children born in each successive month classified as Specifically Learning Disabled." In Hawaii where the cutoff date is December 31st, Diamond found that the December-born (youngest) were twice as likely to be so classified as were the January-born or the oldest. That's double the odds for being diagnosed as Specifically Learning Disabled.

19

Specifically Learning Disabled! Those are strong words; and certainly they carry a stigma for the child upon whom they are placed. For in many cases of youngsters who are having a difficult time achieving, it is clearly NOT a matter of being an LD student, but rather simply a case of physical, emotional and social immaturity, a problem which can easily be cleared up if parents would take our advice and hold back a year.

Oh, that sounds so good and so easy on paper, doesn't it? But when YOU are the parent and YOURS is the child in question, it's doggone hard to read statistics and say, "OK. That sounds pretty good. I guess I'll let him wait a year before starting kindergarten." This is especially so when the child is quite verbal and knows how to count and how to recognize shapes, colors, etc. The situation presents a trap for parents, however, because a child being bright and being ready for school are very different states!

The truth is there are so many factors that enter into the total picture today that it's difficult to make the decision. In a society in which a large number of mothers also hold down full- time jobs outside the home, it's a real relief when that last child, especially, FINALLY gets into school. "And you're asking me to delay that another year!" you might protest.

Yes, we ARE asking you to delay it another year - for the good of that fair-faced youngster of yours, so that the fairness does not turn into a frown because of academic frustrations. We realize, however, that it's tough; for there are many facets to be considered.

One element that clouds the issue is that notorious old IQ score. We (we counselors, that is) call you into the kindergarten screening, sit you down and tell you that your child has an above average IQ. Well, that's just wonderful, you think. You've suspected it all along, of course. But while you're riding high on a parental ego trip, we lay the bomb on you. "Because yours is a **summer child,** we are suggesting you wait a year before enrolling him in kindergarten."

Now this just doesn't make sense, you respond, either vocally or inwardly. Here's a kid with an above average IQ and you're being told he should wait a year before starting school. It seems illogical. Well, you might find the results of our research in this area also to fall into the category of "That Just Doesn't Quite Make Sense to Me." In essence, we have discovered that these **summer children** who prone to academic failure and other school-related trauma are, in the majority of cases, ones with high IQ scores. But they were NOT able to perform on achievement tests nearly as well as one might expect. Our data, however, indicate that the held back **summer children** with lower IQ scores tend to do better than expected. For some reason (the critical age of six perhaps) this was found to be especially true for first graders.

Our Wapakoneta study of pupils who took the Iowa Test of Basic Skills verifies this quite dramatically. An examination of the data indicates a major achievement advantage for the held back **summer children**. For the boys, while only 26.67% of the **summer children** achieved at an above average level, 79.17% of the held back **summer children** did so. The held back **summer children** girls in the group had an almost equally large advantage which included no one at the below average level. A significant 27.78% of the female **summer children**, however, achieved at that lowest level.

If you're into numbers and/or tables, you may want to check out the appendix of this book for an overview of these statistics. Even without consulting charts, however, we think the message is pretty clear. And we're not the only ones finding these trends to be true. A relatively recent study (1984) by Steven R. Huff in the Beavercreek, Ohio School District substantiates our thinking.

Huff's report talks of 40 pre-kindergarten youngsters who, during a 1980 screening, were determined to be "at risk" because of their summer birthdays. After parents were given the data and counseled in much the same way that we would have counseled them, warning them of the **summer child** syndrome, 21 of those parents decided to enroll their youngsters anyway. Another 15 decided to hold their children back a year. The remaining four, for one reason or another, had left the school system by the time the data were collected.

A follow-up study in 1983-84 probably made many of those parents of 21 students wish they had paid closer attention to the counseling which had been provided in 1980. For out of those 21 original students, 15 had been retained in either kindergarten, first or second grade! A look at the children who had been held back from starting school showed that ZERO (0) had been retained during those critical, early years of formal schooling.

If that isn't enough to make you at least stop and consider our suggestions, you might be interested in looking at the achievement scores of these Beavercreek youngsters. Again, tables are provided in the back of this book, but for our purposes here we'll keep it simple.

Early during the second grade year these youngsters were required to take the Iowa Test of Basic Skills. Because of the high number of retentions, the early starters had been in school for an average of 24.4 months at the time of testing. The held back **summer children** in the group, however, (you know, the ZERO who had not failed a grade) had been in a formal schooling environment for 18.0 months each. Yet (and we find this not only interesting but right in line with our research) the early starters had been in school more than **six months longer** than the delayed starters, only to score **five months less** in achievement!

If you're technically or scientifically oriented, you might be eating this stuff up. If, on the other hand, you feel as many do - that these days you can find a chart or table to support just about any theory imaginable, no matter how ludicrous it may sound - we ask you to pause a moment and think about yourself, about your past, about persons you know or have known. We predict that you will be able to come up with numerous examples of either family members, friends or classmates from your past who are **summer children** with a history of school difficulty.

Think about those youthful friends whose fairness of face was sometimes darkened with the gloom of academic frustration, criticism or even failure. Think about those who experienced the problems associated with too much, too soon, for too many.

Maybe you are even one of them. Maybe your parents used to say to you. . .

. . . You COULD do so much better

In school if only you WOULD. . .

Truth is, you probably WOULD have done better, if only you COULD have!

Tuesday's Child

"Full of Grace"

"Full Of Grace"

It's difficult, maybe almost impossible, for a small child to appear graceful in the eyes of his teacher when that youngster is constantly being reprimanded for drifting his attention away from the assigned task at hand. But this is the case with many students who are simply not physically ready for some of the disciplines that formal schooling imposes on them. There are many kindergarten students, for example, who are not able to properly hold a pencil because of a lag in the development of fine motor muscles.

How many kindergarten teachers have had to handle the plaintiff whine, "I can't do it!" from children who feel frustrated because they sense and see that they are not able to manage a paint brush as well as their little friend at the artist's easel next to him? Or what about the little fellow who can't yet print his name legibly - even though many of his classmates can? Or the little girl who can't skip because her large motor skills are not as advanced as those of the child next to her in the play circle?

Just as babies don't all begin teething, walking or talking at the same age, young children are not all going to be ready for school at the same age just because they have turned five - the magic age which our educational system has deigned is the time to be in kindergarten. (Actually, in many states the youngster can be as young as four years, eight months or younger with early testing and still be eligible to start kindergarten.) But a child's readiness for school doesn't just happen automatically. There are numerous factors to be considered, from physical readiness through emotional and social maturity. Subsequent chapters will examine emotional and social growth; for now we'll take a look at the basic question of physical readiness.

You can surely predict what we're about to say: Those six months from five years, zero months to five years, six months can make a world of difference. Well, you're right. We're going to get out the old

25

Victrola and play that worn record again - because, by golly, it's true! Children at that age can develop dramatically in six months in the physical realm. What's more, they can fluctuate between states of inwardized and outwardized behavior, something noted child psychologists Louise Bates Ames and Frances L. Ilg (of the famous Gesell Institute of Child Development in New Haven, Connecticut) term periods of "equilibrium and disequilibrium." According to these experts, these swings in behavior take place just about every six months from age 18 months to 5 years, 6 months. (See chart in appendix). But the length of time between equilibrium and disequilibrium grows to at least nine months when the child reaches school age, 5 to 6-and-one-half years old.

In their book *Your Five Year Old*, Ames and Ilg describe some of the physical characteristics of the kindergarten age youngster. Between 5 years, 6 months and 6-and-one-half years old, for instance, they say, ". . . the child frequently loses his visual orientation and may often reverse his numbers or letters. (This is one of the several reasons why we feel this is not a good age to teach reading or writing. . ."

If normal vision difficulties are causing clumsiness, then children of this age may certainly not see themselves as "full of grace."

Ames and Ilg also call this period one of physical disequilibrium when many colds, headaches, foot aches, face aches and toileting accidents occur. Motorwise, there is more restlessness, less composure and more apparent clumsiness (You know, the old "he can't walk over a piece a string without tripping over it" thing.). It appears that at this age it becomes increasingly difficult for the child to sit still for long periods of time. As the youngster approaches age six-and-one-half years, however, things begin to even out and there is a swing toward a more stable physical state of equilibrium. It would seem logical, then, that for most children, the closer they are to age six when entering a classroom situation which requires a degree of physical maturity, the more successful they will be.

Children who, because of lack of physical grace, experience problems with simply moving through space (as well as with academic learning) often develop negative self-images. Even though they eventually outgrow the physical awkwardness, the emotional scars may not be so quick to disappear. In some severe cases, they may even last a lifetime.

In *Your Five Year Old* Ames and Ilg borrow from educators John J.

Austin and J. Clayton Lafferty who offer some pretty practical clues to a child's kindergarten readiness. They propose a simple list of questions which any parent can check out to determine whether or not the youngster in question is ready for the kindergarten experience. The full list includes 43 questions; but Ames and Ilg publish the nine questions which Austin and Lafferty consider the most significant. According to the educators, if your child is ready for kindergarten, then you should be able to answer yes to most of these:

1. Will your child be five years, six months old or older when he or she begins kindergarten? (You can guess that we really like this question; and note that they list it as number one.)

2. Can he tell you the names of three or four colors that you point out?

3. Can he draw or copy a square?

4. Can he name drawings of across, square, circle?

5. Can he repeat a series of four numbers without practice?

6. Can he tell his left hand from his right?

7. Can he draw and color beyond a simple scribble?

8. Can he tell what things are made of, such as cars, chairs, shoes?

9. Can he travel alone in the neighborhood (two blocks) to store, school, playground or the home of friends?

While Austin and Lafferty certainly consider their checklist important for the kindergarten age child, it also sets the scene for their follow-up list of first grade readiness skills. We find it interesting, as well as gratifying, to note that once again their first question deals with the age of the child, particularly as it references readiness for that crucial skill of reading. Heading their checklist is this one: **Will your child be six years, six months old or older when he begins first grade and starts to receive reading instruction?**

Similarly, in a 1983 syndicated (*Newsday*) newspaper article, John Hildebrand, too, discusses the subject of readiness for kindergarten. Once again, he leads off with the question: **Will your child be five**

years, six months or older when he begins kindergarten.

Are you getting the feeling that this is becoming a popular question in pre-kindergarten circles? Apparently, we aren't the only ones who see the significance in holding a child back until he has arrived at this stage in life, a time when it appears he is more equipped to handle the various situations that arise in a formal classroom structure, a time when a child is more "full of grace" (or at least moving toward that state) than he might have been six months before.

This basic notion of physical readiness is significant in the question of on/off task behavior in the classroom (the ability to concentrate on the assigned task at hand), a skill which does require a certain amount of "grace" on the part of the student. Unfortunately, not all youngsters, **summer children** in particular it seems, measure up. Some simply cannot keep in step. Take Kenny, for instance.

"This young fellow was referred to me (Gilmore) when he was in the fourth grade. Having a September 25th, birth date, the student was nine years, six months old when I met him for the first time. The official reason for the referral was 'behavior problems at home and at school.' While Kenny had previously been found to possess 'average' ability, his skill levels revealed themselves to be slightly below the level expected for his grade placement.

"My notes from our first visit reveal some of his personality traits:

"Kenny talked constantly during the evaluation and seemed to be interested in just about everything. He did show a great deal of concern for the correctness of his responses, asking, 'Is that right?' after many of his answers. This lack of self-confidence was noted in his human figure drawings, also.

"Kenny's psychological file revealed that there were also problems at home. The child had an 18-year-old brother. His father, who had dropped out of school prior to his high school graduation, owned his own business and his mother was going to school to become a nurse. The nine-year-old seemed to be in trouble no matter where he turned. It appeared to be a no-win situation for him.

"I recommended that positive reinforcement, rather than the kind of negative response he was used to getting, be encouraged and that

28

all who dealt with him attempt to spend more time with him in enjoyable activities.

"While Kenny's situation certainly didn't reveal anything that a school psychologist would look upon as unusual or startling in nature, I did have quite a surprise when I visited his classroom. To my amazement I found that there really were no more problems with Kenny than with many of the other students in the class. Some notes I jotted that day paint a vivid picture:

"It was a warm day and the lesson was not that interesting to many of the students. The trip to the music room was a fiasco with the TV program not coming in and no alternative plan evidenced beyond the music teacher talking and the children expected to sit and quietly listen.'

"In a conference with the classroom teacher, I learned that many of her students and those of the other fourth graders in that building were 'immature.' In fact, the problem was so evident that it had been suggested that perhaps the fourth grade teachers should have some special materials for the next year since this particular age group of students appeared to need special attention and help, the teacher told me.

"In reality it was next year's fifth grade (those same children) who would once again need help. It had nothing to do with the age level in general, but rather with the specific children who happened to land in that problem-plagued fourth grade. It seems that a simple misdiagnosis of the situation had taken place. The teachers involved surmised that the problem was with the curriculum; and so new materials were ordered for the next year's fourth grade. But I suspected this would not solve the problem.

"When I examined the records of these fourth graders, my suspicions were confirmed. A good many of them had birthdays in July, August and September. That fourth grade was overloaded with **summer children."**

It might have been classroom situations similar to this one in the midwest that led Louise Bates Ames (co-founder of the Gesell Institute of Human Development) to remark (in 1983):

"Perhaps half our school failures could be fixed if we started children in school when they're ready.

29

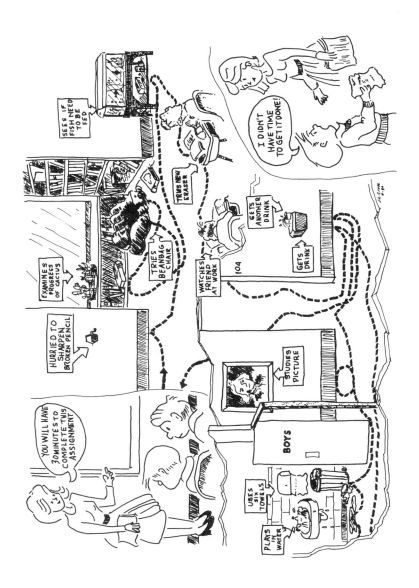

30

Kindergarten requires children to sit quietly, to take turns, to work with workbooks and ditto sheets. But a lot of children at that age need more freedom to move around to play."

It is on the heels of this remark that Ames makes her statement that boys, especially, should be five years, six months old before entering kindergarten. Not that little girls should be excluded from this recommendation. Both sexes should have the opportunity to appear full of grace in their classroom full of peers.

In a 30-minute observation of a kindergarten room, Uphoff kept track of the pupils who got out of their seats without teacher permission. Afterward, he found that **every** child (100%) who was out-of-seat without permission had a summer birthday!

The professionals who support us in this theory have, most likely, observed classroom situations similar to those we have encountered in our research. Extensive study, in fact, by many psychologists and scholars has proven that academic learning time (ALT) is highly correlated with a student's achievement and skills in any one given subject area. In other words, the easier a subject or task is for a student, the more he will learn in any one given period of time. Makes sense, doesn't it?

Unfortunately, ALT is often reduced by events which are beyond the control of the student - fire drills, assemblies and programs, PA announcements, teacher disorganization, lost materials, off-topic discussions, poor discipline, etc. Most teachers, of course, are aware of these problems and are working to improve things. It has also been shown, however that individual youngsters can contribute to ALT by their own attentiveness to the task at hand or they can reduce ALT by daydreaming, talking, doodling, sharpening pencils, etc. It was such off-task behavior patterns as the latter that we have examined in detail.

Each classroom in the Nebraska study, for example, (grades kindergarten through five) was observed for three separate sessions of about 20 minutes each. The sixth graders were observed twice for about 30 minutes each time. These observations occured within a three-week time period; and the classes were involved in large-group math study - one of the skill content areas for which ALT is so crucial.

In order to reduce the chance for unintentional observer error which could occur most easily if the names of the youngsters were used, each student was given a number. Seating charts had numbers instead of names; and the data were entered onto cumulative tally sheets only after all observations were completed for a given class.

"Every 10 seconds I (Uphoff) visually scanned the classroom, noting any off-task behavior by making a tally (⊮╫╫ I I) in the appropriate space on the seating chart. A total per cent of off-task behavior was then calculated for each student for the combined observations

"I then rank ordered these individual 'scores' of off- taskness by boys and by girls with the highest per cent of time off-task being listed first; the lowest, last. I then divided each list into thirds and scores were identified as being SC (**summer children**) and HBSC (held back **summer children** - see chart)."

The differences between the two groups are easily seen. Well over 40% of both summer boys and summer girls were within the most undesirable one-third of the class - those who were found to be the most off-task, the most inattentive. As you have probably already predicted, the youngsters who had been held back were much less likely to appear within that one-third segment of students.

The difference between the **summer children** and the held back **summer children** (in the case of on/off task behavior) is most evident for girls, it seems. The chart clearly shows the value of being an older student in the classroom. For 41.03% of the summer girls were in the highest off-task group, while a mere 11.11% of the held back girls show up in this inattentive segment.

Even for boys the difference in favor of the held back **summer children** is sizeable - 45.83% versus 23.50%.

On the other side of the coin, the data presented in rows C and D of the chart focus on those youngsters who were observed to be the most on-task. They are ranked in the lower third of their class on distractibility and other typical off-task behavioral traits. Parents of **summer children** will be happy to learn that one-fourth of the summer boys and girls were in this "best" group. Obviously, then, some **summer children** are able to find success.

Many more of the held back **summer children**, however, were found to be in this most desirable, lowest off-task group. The girls

(44.40%) did better than the boys (35.30%) who barely exceeded the pure chance score of 33.33 %.

To break down these cumbersome statistics into a more easily digested table of information, the individual per cent of off- task scores for both boys and girls within each group were totaled and a mean (average) score was obtained. These means are also shown in the accompanying table.

Before perusing those stastistics, it should be noted that when a child lacks the coordination (or grace, if you will) to hold a pencil properly, for instance, then that pencil lead is going to break more frequently, thus requiring more sharpening and more seeming disruption. In other words, lack of grace DOES create problems for these children who come up in the negative end of the statistics.

While such numbers and statistics may be useful tools for the researcher or may even be somewhat interesting to the parents and/or teachers of **summer children**, the case studies of these youngsters themselves are much more significant in terms of dealing with the frustrations of a child who simply cannot stay on-task in the classroom, the student who has a hard time keeping in step. Eight-year-old Brian was one such **summer child**.

Born on July 3rd, Brian entered this world about seven weeks prematurely. He obviously had three strikes against him from day one. As he matured, it was apparent that he was fighting an uphill battle. To begin with, he was physically small for his age. He had poor muscle control; or at least it never seemed to be as good as that of his peers. He even had to wear special shoe braces at night to help give him the support that other youngsters his age had naturally and took for granted.

Brian was a likely candidate to be a problem child when he was ready to enter formal schooling. And he certainly didn't disappoint anyone who had made this prediction. During his first four years of school (K through third grade) he appeared to be your typical hyperactive child. He was jumpy, fidgety and had a short attention span. His teachers consistently criticized that Brian's biggest problem was his inability to sit still long enough to complete his work. In other words, he was chronically off-task. His first two years of school in California were problem-filled. When his family moved to Virginia, he was re- enrolled in first grade.

Working together in Brian's school in Virginia, a very

understanding principal, concerned teachers and tutors and the youngster's parents came up with a number of suggestions to help make school life bearable for Brian and to help make Brian bearable to the others in the classroom. Afterall, children who cannot walk up and down a school aisle without bouncing into desks can make academic life difficult for all concerned.

To help everyone cope, Brian's teachers would often simply let him walk out of the classroom when he found that he could no longer contain his excess and disruptive energy. It was explained to him that it would be HIS decision to move out of the room when he felt the need. This participation in his own problem and solution and the permission to exercise some of his own power in the matter seemed to improve his personal control somewhat. As his self-esteem was elevated to a degree (because punishment had been replaced by this more democratic method of dealing with the problem child), his attention span, too, seemed to increase - albeit ever so little.

Obviously this democratic form of dealing with the problem would not work in ALL classrooms. It would take quite understanding teachers, as well as students. But for Brian, at least, it was a start.

While such cases might not seem too unusual today, 20 years ago (when this all occured) the request to repeat a grade (when a student had not "failed") was practically unheard of. Yet, Brian's parents had the foresight and gumption to push for it; and they were victorious.

The epilogue to Brian's story is a happy one. He became the only one of the family's children to complete college (even though two of the other youngsters had been in accelerated classes during their schooling!); and today he is making a successful living working in corporate finance.

There are presently classrooms full of off-task children - much like Brian was in his early years of schooling. Some plug along, barely squeaking by academically and generally just making nuisances of themselves, annoying the more serious students. Others are fortunate enough to have concerned parents and teachers astute enough to detect a problem and attempt to correct it. When this happens, the benefits to the youngster are more significant than just higher grades and fewer punishments.

For when a child begins - for the first time in his young life - to experience success, positive feedback and personal fulfillment, his entire self-image changes. And this, of course, is far more important than being in the upper third of the class or receiving the "most cooperative student" award for the year. This new state of grace, this positive self-image can make all the difference in the world.

Take Lynn, for instance, who was born on June 14. Although her parents divorced shortly after her birth, her natural father stayed in touch with the youngster, even after her mother remarried when Lynn was three 3 years old.

From the first day she entered a classroom, the little girl's teachers could see they had a challenge on their hands. While she was not necessarily the class clown or troublemaker, Lynn was simply unable to concentrate on the assigned task - no matter what it was. With special assistance from her teacher, however, she was able to get through first grade - barely. It was evident that another academic year of this nature would be disastrous to her. But Lynn was caught in a power struggle. While her mother and stepfather half-heartedly agreed that she had been placed in first grade too early, her biological father was vehemently opposed to her repeating the year.

Lynn then spent her entire second grade in much the same state, being labeled a chronic daydreamer by her teachers. Finally, at the end of that year, all parents concerned agreed to let her repeat second grade. That did the trick.

Once she began to feel comfortable with her position in the classroom and with the work load, the youngster became a different student altogether. Being more familiar with her work the second time around, she began to experience positive feedback, success. And she loved it. Lynn was no longer the classroom dreamer. The blank stares gave way to vibrant, interested eyes. The fair-faced youngster who had once been considered so academically awkward was now, in the eyes of her teachers, a child "full of classroom grace."

After quite a successful completion of second grade (for the second time), Lynn was questioned about school. Her response indicated that she was happy that she had repeated the grade.

"You know," she commented quite seriously, "I didn't THINK I was stupid!"

So it wasn't a question of attitude and desire, but rather of readiness. She had experienced the problem of too much, too soon, for too many.

Once again, it was not so much a case of a **summer child** who COULD have done better if only she WOULD have buckled down, but rather one who WOULD have. . . if only she COULD have!

Wednesday's Child

"Full of Woe"

"Full of Woe"

"With your permission, Mr. and Mrs. Parent, we would like to place Jason in our Learning Disabled program. We feel that there he would receive the type of instruction and assistance which would...."

"Learning Disabled?" you say to yourself unbelievingly, not even hearing the description of the program the counselor is recommending for your first grader. "There's nothing wrong with Jason," you tell yourself. "He's normal; he's not below average. He doesn't belong with the LD kids."

"The LD kids." The term has come to carry a stigma - particularly to many parents who would go to great lengths to keep their children from being placed with this group of youngsters who, for one reason or another, just can't quite cut it in school. They need the extra help, the extra attention, the extra little pat on the back to keep them moving and producing. Yes, to be "put in LD" as the children say, is indeed looked upon as "bad news" by many.

While no one likes to admit it, the plight of the learning disabled child (or slow learner, as he is sometimes inappropriately called) is a monumental one. In its 1983 report, "A Nation at Risk: The Imperative for Educational Reform," The National Commission on Excellence in Education recommends the following:

The time available for learning should be expanded through better classroom management and organization of the school day. If necessary, additional time should be found to meet the needs of slow learners...."

No one knows more about these needs than the frustrated parents of children who have been diagnosed as Learning Disabled. Todd's folks are a good example. At the end of his first grade year, Todd had been selected as an alternate for the Advanced Placement Program at his elementary school. His selection was based not so much on his academic grades for the year (which were basically Bs and Cs,) but rather on his above average IQ (He had one of the highest in his class.) and his inquisitive mind and questioning nature.

During the summer one of the students chosen for AP moved out of the district; so Todd was moved into his place in September. When report cards came out at the end of the first quarter and Todd's grades were down to low Cs, his parents were a bit concerned, but reasoned, "If he weren't in the Advanced Placement class, we'd really be worried." But at that point they figured he simply needed a period of adjustment and would eventually catch up.

Before the end of the second quarter, however, Todd's parents were called in for a conference by his regular classroom teacher (not the AP instructor with whom he spent only one hour a day). Not only was he sinking fast in the AP work, but his regular classroom work had fallen well below average.

To make a long story short, Todd was pulled from the AP program and, after some testing by the school counselor, was recommended for the LD program. In just a few short months he had moved from AP "down" to LD! It took two academic years with a tutor to get the youngster to where he was beginning to once again work up to his high potential. But it was only a beginning - and a slight one, at best.

When Todd entered sixth grade the tutor was taken away because he "tested out" of the tutorial program. He continued to plug along, but still at a sluggish pace. His teachers, once again, began describing him as "immature." As long as he had the tutor to "spoon feed" him, he worked. Once this mother figure was eliminated, he was no longer motivated to produce.

The trend continued into junior high school. After the first quarter report cards came out (and Todd was still pulling quite substandard grades for his ability) his parents decided to put him back into the sixth grade. At the time of this writing, Todd is adjusting to the change.

We're sure you won't be surprised to learn that, yes, Todd is a **summer child** with a May 31st birthday. He is but one example of countless young students who are annually diagnosed as Learning Disabled, sending many parents into a tizzy and implanting a low self-esteem notion in many of the children themselves. Face it. Kids are sharp. They know who in their classrooms are classified as the "smart ones" and the "dumb ones."

Fortunately, results of contemporay research are beginning to make parents realize that it's not a case of "smart" and "dumb." There are studies, for example, that confirm a relationship between early school entrance and later diagnosis as Learning Disabled. One such project was undertaken by Dr. Stanley L. Swartz, Associate Professor in the Department of Special Education at Western Illinois University.

His spring, 1984 report concludes, "Such evidence suggests the need to view early school entrants as high risk for a learning disability. Based on these findings a delay in school entrance should be considered a viable preventative intervention strategy."

"These findings" of his and his two assistants (graduate student Kathryn Joy and research assistant Gail Block) are certainly interesting enough to make one sit up and take notice. His subjects were 95 elementary school children (ages six - 12) from a rural west central Illinois school district. Fifty students in standard education programs were selected at random from the entire student population. Forty-five students diagnosed as Learning Disabled and placed in special education programs constituted a sample of the whole.

Permanent school records were used to verify school entrance age and student status (as either standard or LD). The youngsters in the study were then grouped by the age at which they entered kindergarten. The three-month ranges and the age of school entrance were as follows: December to February (ages five years, eight months to five, six); March to May (ages five, five to five, three); June to August (ages five, two to five, zero); and September to November (ages four, nine to four,11).

Can you guess what's coming? Swartz's report states, "A significant relationship between birth quartile and program placement was found. It was noted that the largest grouping contained 20 learning disabled students with late birthdays (September - November)." (See chart for overall look at these results.)

The Swartz report concludes with a number of implied cautions and recommendations:

"Even a cautious interpretation of this study and prior research allows the following conclusions: 1.) children who are older and more mature experience greater school success than children who are younger and immature, 2.)

early entrants are high risk for later learning problems or a specific learning disability, 3.) mandated age requirements can be viewed as a method to insure school readiness for a majority of children, and 4.) testing can be used to allow earlier school entrance for those children found to have the requisite school readiness skills."

Swartz's study puts some numbers around a notion that many researchers have indicated for years and that many non-professionals have had a "gut feeling" about all along; and that is that those children with late birth dates, those **summer children,** suffer a disproportionate incidence of learning disabilities and can be classified in the high risk range for special education.

Yes, the diagnosis of Learning Disabled or the announcement that your child is a candidate for "special" education can be, and often is, looked upon as a bit of "bad news." From the point of view of a youngster, however, the impact of being put into a special class is generally not as traumatic as "flunking" a grade.

They call it "academic retention" these days; it sounds nicer, almost even desirable (and in many cases, believe us, it IS desirable). But to a young boy or girl in the early years of school, to his or her classmates who know they will be moving on to a higher grade and leaving a friend behind, it is "flunking." And no matter how hard loving parents work to help soften the blow and to keep their child's self-esteem on an even keel, the decision that a child has been held back for a year is, indeed, generally accepted as a chunk of "bad news."

While the votes aren't all in yet as to the value of retaining a young student, there's one thing for certain: the topic of holding youngsters back is itself becoming a hotly debated one in school districts across the country. It wasn't at all unusual, prior to the socially oriented 1960s, for a child to repeat a grade. Then in the revolutionary sixties the philosophy of "social promotion" - moving a child on, despite academic difficulties, in order that he might avoid the supposed "emotional trauma" associated with staying back - gained strong support. But academic requirements are getting tougher; and the no-failure approach is losing many of its enthusiastic supporters.

Nevertheless, the debate goes on. Many educators insist that if academic retention is handled properly and positively it can be a good experience for the youngster. Ames (in *Is Your Child in the*

Wrong Grade?) even cautions, "A child who is not ready for promotion needs to be kept back."

The noted educator advises promoting students according to their behavioral age as opposed to their chronological age. "Overplacing," she warns, "can establish a pattern of failure and discipline problems."

By the same token there is a growing number of parents of **summer children** who are retaining them NOT because of academic failure (Indeed, they may be getting Bs or even better!), but because the children are so very socially immature, so physically tiny and/or so emotionally young.

Others maintain that once a child has entered school, retention does NOT pay clear dividends. In their summer, 1984 report in the *Journal of Learning Disabilities*, Deborah C. May, Ed.D., and Edward Welch, Ph.D., take this stance. After studying 223 children (grades two through six) in a suburban New York elementary school), they concluded that taking three years between kindergarten and first grade (as a result of a Gesell Screening Test) did not seem to help the children.

And while there are those who might side with either position, they still emphasize that retaining (or not retaining) is not enough. You've got to get down to the root of the problem. Why is the child not learning? Why is the child so likely to be full of woe?

There are as many theories to answer those questions as there are ways to fix hamburger. The youngster is lazy or immature; he's a late bloomer (particularly true in the case of boys); he is not motivated by his teacher; he and his teacher have a basic personality clash; he can't relate to his teacher's learning style - he'd do better with sight reading than with phonics. His learning style(s) may not mesh with the teacher's teaching style(s). The list can go on and on (particularly when we begin pointing the finger at the poor "teacher" who is so easy to blame for a young student's problems).

There's one point, though, about which most educators agree; and that is if a child MUST repeat a grade, it can do him the most good and be the least awkward early in the school career. This is also the time when the parents have the most say about retaining a youngster.

As was noted in chapter one, Dan Kaercher (in his article in *Better Homes and Gardens*, June, 1984), reports on the growing trend of academic retention. He points out that such steps are usually taken in the lower elementary grades, particularly kindergarten and first grade. But (and we find this particularly interesting) Kaercher also talks about parents who choose to head the problem off at the pass, so to speak, before their child even begins formal education.

His reference to giving a child "an extra year before starting school" is, of course, right in line with our theories and with our caution statement which urges that no child under the age of five years, six months be enrolled in kindergarten.

But what if your child is well past the age of five; and what if he is floundering in school? How should the issue of retention be handled? First of all, the whole idea should never come as a complete shock. Certainly parents and teachers are observant enough to have picked up trends of difficulty all along. It is rare that a problem of learning should suddenly materialize with no prior signs or warnings.

It is during this period of tell-tale signs that parents should work to establish good communication lines with teachers, administrators, school counselors and psychologists and the family pediatrician. Discussions should be held to determine what, if any, diagnostic tests might be in order to trouble shoot the origin of the problem(s). Perhaps you will consider enlisting the assistance of a speech and/or hearing specialist, an optometrist or a neurologist to rule out any suspected abnormalities along these lines. For example, a large number of children who have 20/20 vision also have developmental eye- control problems which greatly inhibit their academic success.

The important thing is to do SOMETHING. Don't try to rationalize that your child is merely going through a phase and/or that he will outgrow the problem. If, of course, you're dealing with a youngster who is having a RARE difficulty for a few days or even a few weeks, OK. Every student has an "off" day now and then. But you know your child; if the signs have been apparent for months, even years, then you must move into action.

HERE ARE SOME THINGS TO LOOK FOR AS AN INDICATION THAT THINGS ARE NOT GOING WELL IN SCHOOL:

*physical complaints, such as stomach aches or headaches, that do not seem to be related to any physical illness and that seem to disappear miraculously on weekends or during vacations

43

*inability or mood changes at homework time

*a feeling of exhaustion at the end of the school day

*abrupt mood swings, particularly when they occur near the time for the school day to begin

*complaints from teachers that the child is nervous, is "out of it,' daydreams or causes any other problems at school

*obviously, poor report card grades

THERE MAY ALSO BE A NUMBER OF SOCIAL-EMOTIONAL CLUES PRESENT:

*"I'm the last one chosen for teams at recess."

*"Nobody likes me."

*"I don't like to play with the kids in my class."

If, after careful observation, consultation with professionals and discussions among all concerned, you feel that your youngster does not belong in the grade in which he is currently placed, you still do not have to jump to the monumental decision of retaining him. There are options to be explored.

Perhaps your child is a good candidate for supplemental tutoring; or maybe his problems can be ironed out in a summer school program. There's also the possibility that the child's teachers and/or parents have unrealistically high academic expectations. Whichever, the problem needs attention.

Are there indications that the problem seems to stem from a poor relationship with the teacher? If the instructor-student chemistry is a disaster and it's still early enough in the year to make a difference, it is not at all out of line to request a reassignment. While schools are not required to comply with such a request, most will do so willingly - and generally with the full cooperation of the teacher. After all, teachers are human, too; they don't want to deal with a youngster when it is apparent that a basic personality clash exists. Your child's problem may be a simple case of classroom anxiety because of this relationship.

Is a change of schools feasible for you and your family at this time? If you think a smaller, private school would be helpful and it is within your budget, perhaps it would be worth exploring, particularly if it has been determined that your youngster needs the extra helping hand of an adult to supply more guidance and positive feedback during the school day. Maybe such a change in school environment in itself will be helpful. Private and parochial schools sometimes have fewer students per teacher in a classroom than do public schools. It could be that a simple switch of this nature, rather than holding back a grade, will supply the answer. We also know of cases where the switch of schools went from private or parochial to the public school with much success.

This whole question of academic retention is such a debated topic at present that school districts across the country are working on viable options. Highland Park School District 108 near Chicago, for example, is one system which has come up with a "transitional first grade" setup for youngsters who have experienced one year of kindergarten but who do not yet demonstrate the develomental skills needed to enter the traditional first grade classroom.

This class is not a special education offering. Nor is it particularly for children with learning disabilities or with below average intelligence levels. Rather, the pupils who are recommended for the course may have a basic lack of maturity or a short attention span. Perhaps they still lack the ability to work independently or are sluggish in the area of speech development. In some cases they may simply have trouble coping with the environment or relating to the other students. They might be unable to share; or they might exhibit a weak self-esteem.

In other words, they are students who are able - but just not ready - to enter the conventional classroom. The transitional classroom is just giving them time to grow up a little, so to speak.

The Highland Park project began in September, 1980, at Sherwood Elementary School. In a March 31, 1983, newspaper feature in the *Deerfield Review*, reporter Debbie Roberts quotes Dave Robert, director of instruction and program evaluation, who has been evaluating the transitional first grade since its inception. Based on the results of pre-tests, post-tests and teacher observation, Robert has monitored students as they enter first and second grades. He says that the program is "not a cure- all."

It does, however, seem to be showing advantages for the

youngsters. "The bulk of the children returned (to the regular program) without additional services," Robert is quoted in the story. "These children tend not to be the strongest in the class. Most do average or above average work. My strong feeling is that all of the children are doing better in first grade than they would without the transitional (program)."

Perhaps there is such an alternative in your district. The possibility is worth exploring as a significant "woe-reduction" for many children.

If you have exhausted just about any answer you can come up with, if the notion of holding your youngster back seems to be the ONLY answer to the dilemma, if you have made this choice, then your biggest challenge yet lies before you - discussing this "bad news" with your child.

The way the whole idea is presented is crucial. Kids, particularly young children under 10, pick up cues from their parents. If you approach the situation positively, chances are more in your favor that your child will also respond in a positive manner. If you act hurt, disappointed, angry, ashamed, then these emotions will surely be transferred to the youngster. And they certainly won't help mend what is probably already a fragile self-esteem.

Of course, basic to your discussion is to let your child know you love him and that he has your support. You might have to spell out the fact that his social, emotional and/or academic performance (and/or lack of) in the classroom does not change this basic love relationship that you have with one another. Even though you may not understand his classroom actions, this should in no way cloud the feelings you have for him as a person, as your special child. Make clear statements to this effect. Use words, hugs, whatever makes you feel most comfortable. Just make sure your child understands how you feel before you proceed to explain what will be happening in his school life.

When you do present your decision, try to frame it in words that will package the deal not as a punishment, but as an opportunity to gain some time and turn things around so that he may actually excel instead of being stuck on the bottom rung of the academic or social ladder. Explain it as a "break" you and his teachers are giving him. Afterall, everyone deserves "a break today" as the familiar jingle goes. The conversation could even be followed by a trip to a local hamburger outlet as reinforcement of the concept.

46

Above all, listen. Give your child the opportunity to express his feelings - even to show his anger if this needs to be done. Probe his mind to find out what's inside. What's going on in that little head where school is concerned? Perhaps an honest discussion will lead to some suggestions as to how to make the next year a better one. Talk about how he views himself. This is so important to his self-esteem. If he indicates that he sees himself as a failure, look for and talk about all his positive qualities. Look for a special talent which has been given him and capitalize on it. Perhaps he has an outstanding artistic ability. Then look for a Saturday class at an art museum. Get him into something that will make him feel good about himself - sports, Scouts, a gym class at the Y, whatever!

While you need to keep him feeling good about himself, you also need to paint a pretty realistic picture of what's happening. Establish the fact that you EXPECT him to pass next year because you know he will be able to do it; and let him know that you are there to support and assist him in any way you can, because the year coming up may be touchy. Emphasize that you, as a parent, are part of the situation and that working together, you can all use this "extra catch up time" to its fullest advantage. You may be surprised to find that such a realistic approach may even be more reassuring to a youngster than a pat on the back and the old "everything will be fine" routine. Kids are sharp today. They know when we're trying to buffalo them. Put the cards on the table and call a spade a spade. You should both be better off for it.

Speaking of throwing the cards on the table, it is important that other members of the family be included in the situation and realize what is going on. Again, the discussion must be approached positively to avoid sibling name-calling and insults. Explain to other children in the family that this decision has been reached in order to help the student in question through a rough time. Emphasize the fact that "we parents did not know what problems could develop when one starts school too early. Now we all need to pull together to make this a growth experience for every member of the family."

Obviously when the subject of academic retention comes up, that old red pencil is involved. For it is usually the teacher- given grades (as opposed to standardized test scores) which put a youngster in the "failure" column in the grade books. Because teacher-given school marks are frequently based upon such maturity factors as pupil effort, cooperation, responsibility, dependability, initiative and self-control, as well as actual academic scores, part of our study (Gilmore's) looks into the relationship between **summer children** and teacher-issued grades.

As would be suspected, Gilmore's efforts in this area revealed the fact that, yes indeed, **summer children** are more prone to below average instructor-issued grades than are held back (delayed school entry) **summer children**. Conversely, the held-back students are far more likely to receive above average grades from their teachers than are **summer children**.

A quick look at the chart in the appendix gives a clear overview of the situation. While 85.71% of the held back **summer children** were consistently issued what would be considered above average grades, only 54.29% of the **summer children** ranked in this category; and while 17.14% of the **summer children** earned below average grades, only 5.71% of the held-back youngsters did so.

The Wapakoneta study also breaks down the teacher-given grades for both boys and girls. While the picture is quite clear for the boys (80.77% of the held-back males scoring above average grades, with only 46.67% of the summer children fellows doing likewise), the results are much more dramatic for the girls in this phase of the study. Results show that 60% of these summer children girls earned above average grades; but an undisputed 100% of the held-back girls scored in this upper level!

Further breakdowns of average and below average grades for both groups of pupils are presented in the appendix.

These results can be explained or interpreted in many lights. There are clearly many factors, both objective and non- objective, involved in the grades that are given young pupils. In addition to raw test scores, teachers generally count in daily class participation, homework, neatness of completed assignments, punctuality in meeting deadlines, cooperation, interest level, etc.

Unfortunately for the woeful **summer child**, to excel in these categories a student must have attained a certain level of maturity, developed decent study and/or work habits and generally have the emotional self-confidence he needs to see a task through to completion. We say "unfortunately" because it appears that it is the youngest group of children in the classroom - the **summer children** - who fall short in these areas. Naturally this will often transfer over into the grading book and show up in that nasty old red pencil as well as be imbedded in the child's psyche.

Two high school principals recently told us about their separate studies of their respective groups of "problem" students - those who regularly came to the administrators' attention for discipline difficulties. Not surprisingly to us, those high schoolers who had started school at less than five years, six months of age made up nearly 80% of these teen-age discipline- problem populations! Thus, punishment joins grades as part of this "full of woe" child's life.

Yes, the end-of-the-quarter report card time is often a traumatic one for **summer children;** for they are the most likely in the classroom to get the Ds and Fs. They are the ones who will have notes scribbled on the back of the cards under "comments." It is their parents who will read such teacher commentary as, "Sara COULD do better in class if only she WOULD. . ." Woe is Sara!

But we know differently. Sara probably had been forced, like too many, to bite off too much, too soon. And Sara WOULD do better in class if only she COULD!

Thursday's Child

"Far to Go"

"Far To Go"

"We're following the leader, the leader, the leader; we're following the leader wherever he may go. We won't be home 'til morning, 'til morning, 'til morning; we won't be home 'til morning because he told us so. . ."

Remember that song from your childhood? Perhaps you used to skip around, imitating the first kid in line - skipping when he skipped, turning circles when he turned. Following the leader! And what a thrill and honor it was to hold that position among your little friends; or to be the "mother" in "Mother, May I?" Yes, even to YOUNGSTERS in that childhood permission game, the role of the leader is an esteemed one for it denotes a certain element of power and control. And what PARENT doesn't beam with pride when told his child has "leadership qualities"?

We know what you're probably thinking. "They're going to play that old tape again. . . **Summer children** show no leadership; they are merely followers. . . blah, blah, blah."

Well, you're partly correct. We'll cite a couple of studies first to support the premise that the youngest students in the class tend to go along with the crowd rather than initiate activities (afterall, that DOES seem logical, does it not?). But then we'll share some surprising results from our own studies.

As we've indicated in previous chapters, as far back as the 1950s this question of early placement was a hotly debated one. So much so, in fact, that schools in Gross Point, Michigan, were willing to devote 14 years - yes, 14 years! - to an experiment to determine the benefits and/or drawbacks of enrolling above average students in school before they were actually ready age- wise.

A full report, by Paul E. Mawhinney, of that experiment was published in May, 1964, in the *Michigan Education Journal*. The headline on the article gives it away: "We Gave Up on Early Entrance."

To capsulize the findings of those involved in the study - nearly one-third of the early entrants in the program turned out to be poorly adjusted to school; only 1/20 of the group was judged to be an outstanding leader at the end of the lengthy experiment; and nearly three out of four of the students observed were considered ENTIRELY lacking in leadership. In addition (and going back to academic findings again) this report also notes that "approximately one in four of the very bright early school entrants was either below average in school or had to repeat a grade."

About the same time (1963) Margaret E. Gott decided to pursue this topic of early entrance for her dissertation at the University of Colorado. She compared 171 California kindergarten students who were about four years, nine months old (section A) at the time of their enrollment with 171 California kindergarten students who entered school at about the age of five years, nine months of age (section B).

All the youngsters in her study were ranked on a 10-point scale measuring socio-emotional development. Gott concluded that four times as many of the younger students (section A) were in the lowest rank. According to records and faculty reports, the older entrants (B) were consistently judged higher on leadership than were the younger entrants (A).

And in yet another study some 20 years later in 1983-84, Joyce McDaniel reached virtually the same conclusions. Working with youngsters in the Englewood Elementary School (Northmont Schools, Ohio), she summarized, "On the basis of this study, this researcher concludes that **summer children** (those born between May 1st and September 30th, for her purposes of study) do show a lag in mental, social and emotional development at the elementary level. They experience more adjustment problems. . .

"Many of our **summer children,**" she continues, "are not ready for school and experience enough difficulty to cause their retention or referral to learning disabilities classes. . . If a child has a bad start in school, he becomes disillusioned with school and tends to give up. This conclusion is supported by much previous research."

And such "bad starts," of course, leave the children with far to go for success and can certainly keep a youngster from assuming any kind of significant leadership role in the classroom - or so we thought.

53

Remember, we told you we had some surprises for you? Well, here they come.

Up to this point in our study (the point of leadership qualities, social development, etc.), our findings were rolling in quite nicely, more than substantiating our gut feelings about the overall portrait of **summer children.** But then a sociometric survey we used to study some of the personal problems of these youngsters yielded some results which shot a few holes through part of our theory.

Basically, this survey was designed to answer one question - whether or not the rather uncomplicated act of holding a **summer child** back for one more year would make a difference in his dealings with his peers. A seven-item sociometric survey was developed, tested and then given to all pupils in grades one through six in the Hebron, Nebraska, part of the research project. The questions were designed in such a way as to obtain information on how the pupils felt about other students in their own classroom. The items were broken down into positive (+) and negative (-) inquiries.

The students were asked to:

+ **1. Name three of your good friends in this class.**

+ **2. Name three of your classmates with whom you'd like to study.**

+ **3. Name three of your classmates with whom you like to play at recess.**

+ **4. Name three of your classmates who could be put in charge of the room if the teacher must be gone for a few minutes.**

+ **5. Name three of your classmates that you want to have on your team in phys ed or gym class.**

- **6. Name three students who need help in learning how to be have better in class.**

- **7. Name three students who need to learn how to share better with others.**

Questions four and six, obviously, were included to elicit the students' perception on the leadership-responsibility characteristics of their classmates - question four being positive in nature; question six, negative. Had the same individuals been selected for both items, the survey's validity would have been in doubt. This did not occur, however, except on a few individual forms.

The results of this section of the sociometric survey were quite surprising to us. In fact, the numbers for the boys actually rejects our hypothesis. It appears that the held back males actually received 7.76% more negative average votes on behaving better and also were beaten (although less soundly) on being in charge of the room.

The girls, however, were a different story. The typical **summer children** pattern continued with them - the younger females receiving 4.51% more negative votes per person on the average for behaving better. On the question on being in charge, however, (and here's another surprise) the **summer children** and the held back **summer children** were nearly even. (See Table in appendix.)

The results as analyzed, then, indicate no strong overall pattern either for or against **summer children** in this area of leadership; and in answer to the original question, it appears that boys do not benefit in any clear way (leadership-wise) from being older as assessed by this paper-pencil process.

The other items on the sociometric survey - the ones dealing specifically with friendships and peer relationships - will be more closely examined in chapter seven. For while this section of our study did not produce our anticipated results, it did seem to support the old stereotype of girls maturing more rapidly than boys; and it also posed some questions about the feminist quality of education as we know it today. (But more about this in the last chapter.)

Back to the basic question of **summer children** and overall advantages of holding back a year, let's look at that old "Following the Leader" tune from our youth. "We won't be home 'til morning, 'till morning, 'till morning..." the llyrics go. Well in a symbolic sense, many **summer children** never make it back "home" to where they belong, i.e., in the category of "achievers." For once a little five-year-old starts down that long - and often frustrating - road to success, he is pretty much on a set course. Like Thursday's Child, he has "far to go." How he gets there will depend, in large part, on how he starts out.

As many researchers have pointed out (and as common sense would appear to dictate), the youngster who begins his formal schooling with positive experiences, positive feedback, emotional pats on the back for good performance, will have the fuel he needs to continue along that road to achievement. The little fellow or girl who starts out sluggishly, who soon gets sidetracked and entangled in a forest of negatives (you COULD do better if only you WOULD. . .) often never does catch up with the others in the race.

In other words, where the **summer child** is concerned, things often don't get any better. At least this is what we postulated. In an effort to determine if we were, indeed, on the right track, we chose a class of high school juniors in the Troy, Ohio, school system and decided to investigate the effect of teacher-given grades in the high school classroom. You'll probably recall that our own study on teacher-assigned grades (that old red pencil) yielded the expected results that **summer children** were on the low end of the totem poll once again.

The Troy mini-survey supported this original premise. We were granted permission to look at the grades assigned to the 34 eleventh grade students in a high school Advanced Placement English class. (Yes, **summer children** DO get chosen for high academic placement; the crucial point, however, is how they handle it.)

While this mini-survey was not as scientifically conducted as our Hebron and Wapakoneta studies, it did yield some interesting results which certainly supported our theory of the younger students in the class being at a disadvantage - particularly when it comes to something like grades on a nine- week term paper project, which can certainly be subjective to a degree. These papers, however, were graded on a very detailed evaluation system which required an average of 65 minutes grading time per paper from the teacher.

The birth years of the 34 students in the class spanned three - 1966, 1967 and 1968. Thirteen of the pupils were born in 1966; 20, in 1967; and only one in 1968.

This is basically what we found. Taking the oldest 20% of the teen-agers in the class, we learned that 71.4% of those students were given As for their term papers. By contrast, only 14.3% of the youngest 20% were awarded As for their research efforts.

Breaking the stats down even further (and perhaps making it even clearer) - the one lone 1968er (the youngest student) did not earn an A. He did, however, come through with quite a respectable B grade. Of the 20 students born in 1967, six students (30% of the 1967

56

group) earned As; and of those older teens born in 1966, seven (or 54%) pulled the top grades. A complete breakdown of A, B, C and D grades is provided in the appendix. For our purposes, suffice it to say that these numbers jive with what we would have expected. In other words, the younger students DO seem to lag and often do not catch up with their older peers.

Being bright was not the issue here because all were bright. How effectively one uses his or her brightness was. Factors such as being able to plan, organize, provide self-discipline, meet deadlines, etc., are often maturity-related; and without them, even a bright high-schooler often has "far to go."

Notice we said "often." For just about every study conducted in the name of research and/or education, you can find another one to refute the results. In a May, 1980, article in the *Journal of Learning Disabilities*, much attention is given to "The Birthdate Effect," the title of the report. The authors, Glenn W. DiPasquale, Ph.D., Allan D. Moule, Ph.D., and Robert W. Flewelling, Ph.D., address themselves to the question of entry age.

The participants in their study were 552 children in grades K through 12. Just as we have observed in our work, most of their referrals for remedial help (most LD kids) had early, rather than late, birthdates. Most, then, were **summer** or fall **children**. (Fall, because this study was conducted in Canada where the cutoff entrance age date is December 31st.) And just as we have found, the significant effect appeared to be limited more to the boys than to the girls in the study.

While our research stopped with sixth graders, theirs was carried on into the high school classroom. On the basis of what they have observed, the three authors indicate that by the time the student reaches the secondary level of education, he seems to have caught up, regardless of birthdate. This is, indeed, encouraging for those of us who have older **summer children**.

So once again, who (or what) do you believe? Is the **summer children** syndrome lasting? Or can a youngster "outgrow" it? Each answer, of course, is as individual as the child in question. Just how far do they have to go to find well-rounded success?

There is one topic, however, that you won't get too much arguing about these days - the undue pressures and stresses placed on youngsters. Yes, just about anyone will agree that while we certainly desire the best in education for our children, sometimes the traffic on that long road to success just gets crazy. Recently we see more and more trends to ease the stress.

We've already discussed the impetus for this pressure on children to achieve, to learn, to grow up too quickly. The 1957 Sputnik scare created what Anne K. Soderman refers to as a "cognitive sifting down" of curriculum throughout the country. Consequently, what is being taught to most kindergarten children today is what was expected for the first grader 15 or more years ago. And that's not so good. The pre-Sputnik research found that many of those children had problems with the curriculum then. Now that the curriculum is even tougher, many more of the children experience real problems!

From the mid-sixties on, educators started working on various types of non-graded programs for the primary (grades one through three) years. Children were placed in multi-age groups rather than into first grade, second grade, etc. It was a reaction to the problems being experienced by these first children to have to cope with the "sifted down" curriculum.

It was widely acknowledged that as many as 40% of these youngsters would need four years instead of the usual three years to complete, with success, these post-kindergarten expectations. What we see is that many children in the late 1980s continue to need this "extra year" of psychological and developmental growth. And we contend that it is best "taken" **before** starting kindergarten!

Others agree. Bertha Campbell, for instance, head of the Bureau of Child Development at the New York State Department of Education, says that demanding kindergartens create too much stress for the youngsters and can have damaging consequences. Quoted in a *TIME* magazine article (Oct. 8, 1984), she warns, "We have data which say absolutely that if you 'structure' too quickly you kill creative thinking."

Campbell is certainly not the only professional concerned with childhood stress and undue pressures on youngsters. The esteemed American Academy of Pediatricians, in fact, has expressed concern about the dramatic increase of stress-related symptoms being seen in young children. There are, of course, many factors contributing to this relatively new medical phenomenon - high divorce rates, working mothers, economic problems, etc. But we certainly cannot discount the fact that academic pressures play a role in the total picture.

Yes, it's a veritable jungle out there - even in what was once the sheltered world of childhood. With even preschoolers being exposed to the various negatives of our culture via television, video tapes and other media, there's not too much that is hidden from kids today. It used to be that rather precocious children were considered "street wise." Well today there are many youngsters you might term "media wise." By the time they've reached third grade, they've heard and/or seen plenty! Not only do today's children have far to go, but the road is much more difficult to travel.

That's one of the reasons there are individuals, groups, even entire school districts working to help combat the stress such adult knowledge is causing. There is, for instance, an elementary school in Vermont (yes, kids are stressed even in a nice placid place like Vermont!) which is teaching children how to relax their muscles in an effort to cope with stress.

In an Associated Press story issued in the summer of 1984, Derby Line Elementary School principal David Elwood is quoted as explaining, "Kids at the elementary school level certainly have many instances in which stress is placed upon them. . . The stress is there even though they may not have ulcers in the third grade."

About 160 students at Derby Line were offered a 12-week course in which they were taught how to recognize stress. They acted out good and bad ways to respond to stressful situations; and they were also taught muscle relaxation techniques.

And then there's the group out in Racine, Wisconsin. A fledgling organization called Children Need Childhood, they are urging the Racine School Board to lessen the workload for children in kindergarten and the early elementary grades. They, like many others, feel that their children are being asked to learn too much too soon. They believe that somewhat delayed learning will, in reality, be better and longer-lasting. Thus, delaying the start of this "far to go" trip is likely to get one to the end of the trip faster, safer and more successfully!

Recognizing the positive fact that, yes, standardized test scores in their area are indeed up, they ask a more basic and significant question: "Are these students emotionally stable under the pressure?"

Unfortunately, many parents, teachers and physicians throughout the country are discovering that the depressing answer to that inquiry is a definite, "No!" Much to the dismay of administrators who are working to make their schools the best in the district (something which is generally measured, in large part, by standardized test scores), to the teachers who feel they must stick to the curriculum and text books assigned to them lest they get fired and to that segment of modern-day parents who rush their children from the crib to learn their ABCs, there are simply many youngsters who are not geared for life in the fast lane. It's these kids who become overwhelmed by the lightning-fast pace which has become a standard in the 1980s American classroom.

It is often Thursday's Child, the one who has far to go, who crashes in this fast lane where there is just too much, too soon, for too many. It's not that he wants to drop out of the race. He'd like to make it to the end of the road to success; and he WOULD. . . if only he COULD!

Friday's Child

"Loving and Giving"

"Loving and Giving"

What can you say about love? Where do you begin? Ask everyone you know to give you a definition of "love," and you'll probably get as many answers as you would have had you asked them for different ways to use peanut butter. Perhaps that's because the emotion of love is such an individual and personal one. We all show love in varying ways - particularly when it comes to our children. Some of us are physically demonstrative; we like the hugs and the kissy-face sort of encounters. Others of us may appear to be more stoic in our relationship with our youngsters. Yet that certainly doesn't mean we don't love them.

But that's not the crucial issue here. It's not how WE (as parents, teachers and caregivers) show love toward our children. Rather, it's how THEY perceive it. There are, sadly, many youngsters who might be lavished with embraces, showered with toys and other goodies, constantly praised, yet still feel unloved. How can this be, you ask?

It can be because kids are sharp. They can pick up on our feelings, our attitudes, even our body language. You might be responding half-heartedly to your five-year-old's need for a hug while your mind is wandering, wondering how you're going to get caught up with that desk full of work that's awaiting you tomorrow morning or pondering what in the world you can prepare for dinner tonight. You're not zeroed-in on the kid and he probably can sense that.

Or take the child who begs and begs for a new toy. Perhaps you buy it for him just to shut him up and get him out of your way so you can have some peace and time to yourself. It's quite possible that, if this sort of situation is recurring, he will pick up on your feelings and motives.

We could go on and on; and many prominent and noted authors for whom we have the greatest respect (Gilmore always suggests that parents read Dreikurs' *Children: The Challenge)* have done so in countless volumes on child-rearing. If you'd like to pursue the subject we direct your attention to the bibliography at the end of this book.

For our purposes here in dealing with **summer children,** we'd like to make one simple point when it comes to the subject of love. You want to make your child feel loved? The basic solution is simple: Treat him with the respect you hopefuly have for your spouse, your friends, other adults in your life.

Now don't jump to conclusions. We aren't saying you should treat the youngster as you would an adult. That's quite unrealistic and would certainly open a whole new can of worms, as Elkind and Postman have so vividly described in their books. We're merely saying that children are persons. They have feelings, desires, needs; and we (as parents and educators) should tune into them, respecting them as individuals. Just ask yourself this question: If you treated all the adults you know with the same amount (or lack)of respect you reserve for your children, would you have any friends?

We're referring here to such things as name-calling and personal attacks. How many times, for instance, have you found yourself saying something like, "Johnnie, pick up your clothes! How can you stand to be such a slob?" Or, "Quit your whining, Lisa. You are such a baby! When are you going to grow up?" Come on now. Don't be ashamed to admit it. We all spout off like this without thinking. After all, we're only human and our emotional side takes over sometimes - particularly during a period of fatigue. What we're suggesting is that instead of pointing an accusing finger at the child in question, rather point that finger at the "act" which has you bothered. Or even point the finger at yourself. "Dirty clothes on the floor really annoy me, Johnnie. You know that. Now please cooperate. Pick them up and deposit them in the proper place." This is certainly less damaging to a child's self-esteem than the "you dirty slob" kind of statement.

When considering these essentials of love and self-esteem, it's interesting (and important) to note that it is nearly impossible to give what you don't first have. We can cite many sources for this premise. Hebrew Scriptures, for instance, (Leviticus 19:18) address the notion. "Thou shalt not avenge nor bear any grudge against the children of thy people, but thou shalt love thy neighbour as thyself."

Likewise, in Christian Scriptures, Matthew (22: 34 and following) writes, ". . . And the second (commandment) is like unto it, Thou shalt love thy neighbour as thyself."

Even contemporary songs imply this underlying premise. "I can't be right for somebody else if I'm not right for me," are lyrics from the popular, "I"ve Gotta Be Me."

If you are interested in pursuing this topic of developing your youngster's self-image, we highly recommend *Your Child's Self-Esteem* by Dorothy Corkille Briggs. This common-sense author presents practical, step-by-step guidelines for raising responsible, productive, happy children - children with a solid sense of self-worth, children who feel good about themselves. Which brings us back to **summer children.** Above all, we want these kids to feel good about themselves; but oftentimes they cannot because of the negative reinforcement they receive.

We all know how hard it is to break out of a vicious circle of negatives. The kid who starts out sluggishly in kindergarten or the one who becomes known as the class clown from day one, has a terrible time trying to break out of the negative image he has established early on. And we don't help matters any. When a child brings home a lousy report from school, what do we do? Attack him:

"Why don't you use your head?"

"When are you gonna quit wasting time?"

"What's wrong with you, anyway?"

"You COULD do better if only you WOULD. . ."

Such negative parental or teacher comments clearly imply that the child has a bad attitude which is causing the problem. How much better for his self-esteem it would be were we able to sit down with him and attempt to calmly discuss the issue, all the time providing some positive reinforcement rather than negative.

The adult needs to say, "Let's talk about the problem. We can work together to solve it. We both know there's an answer here somewhere. Let's make a pact here and now to work together until we have this thing licked!" Joint efforts aimed at a problem which is, in many cases, more a readiness issue than an attitudinal one are more likely to result in success.

Now if you think we're trying to give the impression that one nice talk like this will take care of things, you're dead wrong. This attitude is merely a beginning. There will, no doubt, be many hurdles for you (as a team) to weather together. But if you can work under the umbrella of respect, of positive reinforcement, then how much better it will be for the emotional health of your youngster. (You won't get as wet, either!)

Most parents, of course, realize the importance of praise for a job well-done. That compliment for your five-year-old when he brings home a finger-painting is so essential for his development as a person. We don't have to tell you that. And, what the heck; it's easy to praise a kid when he runs in the house beaming, proudly displaying his latest work of art. Where it really gets tough is when he comes home from second grade with a math paper that says "missed 14." Talk about the proverbial fan! How do you keep from blowing off? Where does positive reinforcement come in here? How does the focus of readiness fit into the situation?

Believe it or not, there is a place for it. There IS a way in which you can continue to help your child build a positive self-image while also being realistic about his current level of work.

Start the focus on the number of items which were correct. The child already knows how many were missed and doesn't need "double jeapordy." If the youngster is not ready, attitudinally (often caused by lack of success and the blame messages sent by others) and/or developmentally, too much adult involvement at this point can lead to a lifelong dependency on others by the child.

You might want to consider such measures as parent-teacher conferences about readiness or possible retention. Perhaps you could discuss small, step-by-step improvement plans which could include backing off from the current grade level expectations and returning to prerequisite skill development.

Some of this can be instigated at home.

"You know, Jeff, you did well on most of those math problems. It seems you may still need a little extra help with others. Would you like for me to help you? Now, where can we start? We could take 15 minutes each night and go over the flash cards. It's important to learn these basic math facts."

If this were a scene from "The Brady Bunch," the kid would say, "Sure, Mom. That's a GREAT idea! Gee, thanks for taking time from your sewing after dinner. You're swell!"

65

Unfortunately, most of our home environments are a far cry from the atmosphere depicted in such idealistic TV sit-coms. If "Jeff" is anything like your typical second-grader, he'll most likely fight you tooth-and-nail over those old flash cards. He'd probably rather be watching reruns of "The Brady Bunch" after dinner. But as a parent, it is your responsibility to see to it that he does sit down and work with you (or with an older sibling, perhaps). No one said it would be easy. And there will probably be some ugly scenes. But the point is, the child himself does not have to be attacked. It is his action, his attitude perhaps, which is on the firing line. And he must be made to understand the difference. How you explain this, of course, will be an individual thing, based on the personalities and circumstances involved.

You might stop to consider that even we adults tend to avoid, or at least put off, some of those necessary tasks which are for us less easy or more unpleasant. Well so do kids!

Many adults use a system of "self-rewards" interspersed between relatively short time-segments of work on those less easy or unpleasant tasks. Perhaps you reward yourself with a cup of herb tea in the afternoon, after you've completed the laundry or put the finishing touches on a report. Maybe it's a video tape you rent on Friday evening after a productive week at work.

Using this same type of system WITH (not ON) the child will keep the work in small segments, the time per segment manageable and the experience more enjoyable and productive for all. The "reward," of course, must be one which the child values.

For you see, Friday's Child has needs, too. While he may be "loving and giving," he also has a real need to be loved - in the genuine sense. This does not discount discipline on your part as a parent or teacher. Before he can love others, however, he must first learn to love himself, to feel good about himself. When this healthy process does not take place, then we have countless emotional problems.

It is this issue of the emotional maturity of **summer children** that we consider of utmost importance; for a solid basis of emotional stability permeates a child's very being. Without that he can, indeed, be in trouble in all the other areas of his life. Fortunately there are many parents today who are tuned into their child's emotional readiness (and/or lack of). Stephen's folks are a case in point. Stephen could read when he was three, but his kindergarten teacher believed he had a learning disability.

"He didn't get along well with other children and would rather read the ads in the *Reader's Digest* than go out and climb a tree," his mother stated in an interview. Believing then that Stephen (who is actually a gifted child as opposed to an LD student, as his kindergarten teacher had surmised) was not emotionally ready to handle school, his parents held him back a year.

To us, of course, this decision was a wise one. For starting him too early in first grade could surely have detrimental effects on him later - in such areas as decision making, handling stress and being creative. Stephen is just another example of a youngster who can be extremely bright - and, in this case, he surely is - and still not be ready for school.

Some of the questions we give parents on our checklist of criteria for classroom readiness deal with the child's emotional level. We generally advise that if the parents can answer "yes" to these, then the youngster should probably be held back a year. (There are, of course, other questions on the checklist - which appear in the last chapter of this book. A decision should not be made solely on the basis of the following.)

* **Does the child not enjoy being with other children?**

* **Does the child not share with siblings or other family members?**

* **Is the child shy?**

* **Does the child cry when left alone?**

* **Is the youngster easily frightened?**

While Stephen's mother did not anticipate the same type of problem with her daughter, Regina, she nevertheless found other reasons for waiting to send her to school, too. "I believe in letting a kid be a kid," she commented. "It's so hard to grow up anyway. Why should they be pushed?"

Interestingly enough, that's the same question that was indicated in a *Newsweek* cover story on "Bringing Up Superbaby" (March 28, 1983). A good portion of that extensive feature was devoted to the subject of childhood stress and its emotional repercussions.

67

Minneapolis pediatrician Paul Batalden is quoted in the article, explaining, "I see an enormous amount of pressure on children and it shows up in headaches and abdominal pain. Parents come into my office complaining (that) their child looks peaked or is tired all the time or doesn't feel excited about living anymore."

Doesn't feel excited about living anymore? These are pre-schoolers we're talking about! What a pathetic and ominous comment!

The same *Newsweek* feature also points out some danger signals which are apparent in many families. Chicago psychologist Myra Leifer talks in the article about toddlers (ages two and three) who have been known to pull out clumps of their hair or their eyelashes because of their uncontrollable distress. Other signs of such disturbance, she warns in an inauspicious manner, "may not occur for years."

Houston psychiatrist Angelica Frias elaborates, in the article, on that theory, noting that anorexia nervosa (the much publicized eating disorder) can develop in teen-agers raised in homes that rank intellectual achievement above all else. "A baby can always learn cognitive skills," she warns, "But it's very difficult to go back and redo emotional development."

That's an understatement! It's probably darn near impossible to go back and redo emotional development - not without a lot of professional help and a strong support system from family and loved ones.

This whole question of emotional readiness is especially pertinent when dealing with a youngster at the traditional kindergarten age. Ames and Ilg (in *Your Five-Year-Old*) point out that "emotionally the child of this age may seem to be in an almost constant state of tension. . . tantrum age again." That certainly doesn't sound like the time of life to introduce new stresses and expectations that he just might not yet be equipped to handle.

Inez King (writing in the *Elementary School Journal* as far back as 1955) brought out this point quite succinctly. ". . . having attained a few additional months of chronological age at the beginning of grade one is an important factor in a child's ability to meet imposed restrictions and tensions that the school necessarily presents."

And, again, Ames and Ilg, sing the same tune. "Birthday or

chronological age is no guarantee of readiness for school. Our position is that the child's behavior age, not his birthday age, should determine the time of school entrance and of subsequent promotion. . . A child can be bright for his age and at the same time young for his age. A high IQ does not guarantee school readiness. . . It takes more than a good intelligence for a child to succeed in school. It also requires a certain maturity."

You certainly won't catch us arguing with that! We have stressed over and over that the issue of emotional maturity is probably the most crucial one where our children are involved. We want them to grow up with a postive self-image. We want them to feel good about themselves. And this is where it all begins - at the grass roots emotional level.

But there's also an intellectual reason for the sound emotional basis. While scientists are not exactly sure just how information gets into the brain, they are picking up more and more hints that when an experience (such as an academic exercise) is associated with an unpleasant emotional atmosphere, then the information never reaches the memory bank. If a child, for instance, feels stressed while flipping through those math flash cards or while attempting to read aloud in first grade, if exercises of this sort make him anxious (because he is not mature enough to handle them) then that lesson may never be learned - and consequently, future lessons will be ineffective.

While this may be of particular interest to the teacher in charge, for the parent the basic emotional health of the child is of much farther reaching significance. There have been a number of studies, including our own, which have addressed themselves to this issue. The Oak Ridge experiment described in chapter one is a good one. The 104 children studied in that research project (which, by the way, was conducted back in the early 1950s) were described by their teachers with such phrases as "emotional problem," "facial tic," "bites nails," "cries often,' "asthma" and "unduly nervous." Of the 54 younger children studied in Group One of the project, 19 boys and 16 girls were described by their teachers as having some "undesirable growth characteristic" or were found to be "maladjusted" in some way. Of the older Summer children in Group Two, only six (three boys and three girls) out of 50 were found to exhibit any sort of emotional trauma.

Likewise, the Nassan County Elementary Principals Association project reported by Arthur E. Hamalainen and described in chapter one highlights the emotional issue. "The disparity between groups (of **summer children** and held back **summer children**)," the report points out, "becomes more evident in emotional adjustment, where 94% of the (school) principals report that the under-age child commonly faces problems in this area.

"In general," the report concludes, "it may be deduced from this table that the under-age child has greater problems of adjustment in all areas except scholastic achievement in grades four through six. It is particularly in the areas of social and emotional adjustment that the under-age child is at the greatest disadvantage and this disadvantage persists through all grades. The over-age child fares better than the under-age boy or girl while the average-age child is the best adjusted according to the principals' reports."

In yet another experiment conducted in the early 1960s for the Highline School District in suburban Seattle, the same results were obtained. The study compared the achievement of selected pupils who were admitted to school early. The findings generally indicated that pupils who entered early on the basis of high scores on intelligence or mental age tests achieved above the level of those who were not allowed to enter early, as they well should have since they were brighter! These bright children who did enter early, however, had more than the average number of social and emotional problems - even into the secondary school scene, the study found.

And carrying the emotional trauma question even beyond the high school years, a Montclair, New Jersey study came up with these ominous conclusions: ". . . those pupils who were very bright but very young at the time of school entrance did not realize their potential. They tended to be physically immature or emotionally unstable, or they would cry easily."

And socially, they seldom showed leadership. (See the previous chapter in this book). From junior high school on, 50% of them earned only C grades. On the other hand, generally the very bright late-school-entrance group excelled throughzout their school careers. . . in many cases early entry may result in maladjustment in school, and even may have an adverse effect on **ADULT LIFE**." (Those bold caps are ours.)

"On **ADULT LIFE**," they prophesy. Those are ominous words, indeed. But they are intriguing words. How many adults today, do you suppose, are regularly visiting analysts because of some unresolved emotional issue from their youth? How many of us today

70

(particularly us baby-boomers) are the emotionally-tipsy products of well-meaning parents and teachers who jumped right on the bandwagon back in the fifties, pushing us to excell, to learn, to succeed, to grow up! And how many of us might have, indeed, memorized all the required formulas and theorems and picky gramatical rules, but perhaps have never quite matured emotionally? How many of us really do feel good about ourselves?

When push comes to shove, isn't that what it's all about? Feeling good about yourself? Having children who can take pride in themselves for the individuals they are, not for the grades they might bring home? Raising a generation of youngsters who can look within themselves and discover a blessing or talent (however meager it may seem) and go out and DO something with it? Positive reinforcement. It's one of the buzz words of the '80s. But it is, oh, so essential to the emotional health of any human being, no matter what age.

It is, perhaps, a conspicuous lack of such emotional stability which contributes to such threatening newspaper headlines as the following:

*More young people feel despair, kill selves

*Teen suicide: a national epidemic?

*Recognizing the warning signs of teen-age suicides

Frightening as they may seem, headlines such as these appear in newspapers and magazines throughout the country with an alarming frequency these days. You may even recall reading of a high school in Texas where a half dozen or so students committed suicide within a span of just a few weeks. Statistics have indicated that one out of every three teens contemplates suicide at some point during their young adult years. In 1983, more than 5000 United States teen-agers took their own lives. It is estimated that well over 6000 will die in 1986. Their motives vary.

For one 14-year-old Ohio girl, for instance, a broken love affair became a matter of life and death. She chose the latter. "I'm going to prove my love for him. I'm going to take my own life. . . Maybe then he'll love me and want me," the teen-ager wrote in a letter which was published in an account in the *Dayton Daily News*. Almost two months later the young lady did commit suicide by ODing on drugs.

Unfulfilled affairs of the heart are but one motivation for young people today to contemplate ending it all. We don't have to recite the litany for you. You know it by heart by now - drug and alcohol abuse, broken and unstable family situations, undue pressures in school, at home, on the work scene, economic problems. Take your pick.

But the world has been plagued with such ills for generations. Our parents - and their parents before them - had to deal with monumental crises and tragedies, with daily problems, frustrations and setbacks. Why is it we didn't hear of so many young adult suicides in those days? For it is true, the rate is rising dramatically.

According to national statistics released by the Dayton (Ohio) Suicide Prevention Center - in 1960, there were 3.6 suicides per 100,000 youths, ages 15 to 19. By 1980, that figure had risen to 8.5 suicides per 100,000 in that same age group. For every 100,000 persons in the 20 to 24 age bracket, there were 7.1 suicides in 1960. By 1980, that tally had risen to 16.1. That's more than double!

The whole issue of teen-age suicide is such a bizarre one. Why would anyone in the prime of life, when they are potentially just beginning to experience the fullness of living, want to die? It's a question that even the survivors often cannot answer.

It was a quote from Anne K. Soderman which led us to begin our own investigation of the effect of too early a school entrance on later teen-age suicide. "Children at four or five," Soderman writes, "have a genuine need to play and the quality and quantity of the time they spend playing are later seen (or observed to be lacking) in their creative thought, ability to make decisions, and potential for coping with stressful situations."

These children in high academic curriculums have little time for play, it's true. Could this have been partially responsible for the increase in youth suicide in the United States in the last 20 years? It is a question which we continue to investigate at this writing.

At this point, however, even many of the families of the teen victims are still asking, "WHY?" A *Dayton Daily News* feature (May 7, 1984) quoted Mrs. Wanda Johnson, who heads the Dayton Suicide Prevention Center's survivor outreach program. She is well-equipped to handle the calls that come through, as she lost her 17-year-son to the suicide syndrome. "I lost my teen-age son four years ago, at 17. As far as an answer to why, that is the most puzzling thing," she is quoted as saying.

"The reason my own son gave was that he thought he was failing in school, that he wasn't going to be able to win a scholarship he had in mind," she explains in the feature. "If that was the real reason, I don't know. But that's the way he explained it in his note."

Mrs. Johnson refers to a problem period which she was aware of, but thought it was merely a phase her son would outgrow. "We visited the school," she said, "and they were as much in the dark as we were. They thought it was just a phase he was going through."

You don't have to look far for articles on warning signals or for advice on how to handle teen-agers who might appear suicidal. Most of these accounts agree on many points, including the essentials of life which are generally missing from the lives of the young people who do attempt to take their own lives. An article by Peg Weaver in the June 6, 1984 *Lutheran* magazine ties it all up quite nicely:

"Several factors are usually missing from young potential suicides. Without the factors - self-esteem, family trust and responsibility, discipline, and opportunities to solve problems for themselves - teens are likely to experience not only more crises but also more severe ones.

Self-esteem is more than pride. It has to do with a feeling of adequacy to cope with daily life. Some young people have more difficulty than others dealing with the criticism or teasing of parents and friends."

Again, self-esteem (or more appropriately, a lack of a positive self-image) is generally pinpointed as one of the tragic culprits in cases of many young suicides. Because we feel so strongly about the importance of youngsters feeling good about themselves and because of the results of our study of **summer children** thus far, we decided to examine the question of **summer children** and suicide. At the time of this writing, our data are scant; but the results so far are intriguing.

Using 1983 and 1984 data provided by the Montgomery County (Ohio) Coroner's office, we examined the files of 28 persons under the age of 26 who committed suicide between January 1, 1983 and June 30, 1984. We found that five of the six women who took their own lives were born in the summer. Ten of the 22 males studied were also **summer chidren.**

Translated into more technical terminology, we find that 83% of the female victims and 45% of the male victims had birthdays between June and September. A normal distribution would have been 33%. We feel strongly that all of these young suicides would have been children who entered school at an early age since the practice of holding back less mature youngsters is a relatively recent development.

The results are intriguing enough to us that we keep asking ourselves the question triggered by Soderman's comment on the lack of play at early ages. Can this lack of play at ages four and five later lead to an inability to cope with adolescent and young adult problems?

In addition, we are attempting to gather similar data from coroners throughout the country. Should these results continue to hold up after further research, they will provide yet another major reason for parents to hold back their "too young" children one more year before starting them in school.

Should we be able to gather the information and obtain the results we anticipate, we will add yet another segment of frustrated, and now departed, young people who WOULD have felt good about themselves, who WOULD have attempted to make the most of their God-given talents, skills and virtues, who WOULD have clung fiercely to the very fullness of life which was theirs for the taking. . . if only they COULD have.

Saturday's Child

"Works Hard For a Living"

"Works Hard For A Living"

Have you ever had the misfortune to be stuck in a nasty snow storm-sitting in a pile of the stuff, your automobile wheels spinning furiously, yet getting you nowhere?

Or have you ever spent an entire day in what seemed like constant movement - busy with this, that and the other - but really unable to point to any one major accomplishment for your efforts?

We've all experienced frustrating situations like these. That's why it's easy for us to identify with the child, particularly the summer child, who seems to be forever spinning his wheels in school, yet getting nowhere. To add insult to injury, what he perceives as hard work is, most likely, earning him nothing but negative feedback from his teachers and parents. The harder he works, the more worthless he is made to feel because his academic performance is below par.

Whether the child is bright (but labeled an underachiever) or of normal IQ (but must struggle) makes little difference to the youngster. All he perceives is that he's "working hard for a living," but with little - or no - reward.

It sounds like a "no win" situation; and, unfortunately, in many cases it is. For the wheels just keep spinning. - grade after grade, year after year, even into adulthood - unless the basic problem can be attacked and eliminated.

Scott is a **summer child** who found himself in this position at age nine; but his story is a bit different from the typical under-age youngster. With a late July birthday he was, indeed, one of the very youngest in his kindergarten class when he entered a formal education setting at the tender age of five years, six weeks. Having had two years of preschool previously, young Scott had no problem

76

whatever adjusting socially. Plus, his outgoing and friendly nature helped him become one of the most popular youngsters in the classroom. Even his kindergarten teacher had to admit to his parents that the well-behaved little boy was one of her favorites.

Add to these qualities an above-average IQ (not uncommon for a **summer child**), a photogenic face which looks as if it belongs on the cover of a magazine and a smile which would melt your heart, and you'd think, "This kid's got it made."

Well, you'd be correct - at first. In kindergarten, even into first grade, Scott had everything going for him. At the end of his first grade year, in fact, he was chosen for the advanced placement class - not necessarily on the basis of grades alone, but because he had so much potential for learning and appeared to be a "serious" student. Again, his first grade teacher told his proud parents the same thing they had heard the year before. "Scott is so mannerly. He's a joy to have in class."

Unfortunately, it was this well-behaved countenance that may have been mistaken for the "serious student" tag which was placed on the youngster. For a more astute teacher in second grade began to have motivational problems with him. Because the work load was heavier than the curriculum imposed in first grade and because more was expected of the child individually, Scott began to falter a bit. While he was by no means on the brink of failure, his above average work was falling. His As and Bs were turning into Cs and even an occasional D.

A look at Scott's records and interviews with his teachers give a pretty clear indication of the problem - he was simply disorganized. Both his classroom teacher and his advanced placement instructor were imposing challenges which required him to do some organizing and quite a bit of independent work. He was even required to do a brief "research paper" using the library facilities. It seemed that it was assignments such as these - where there was no teacher there to guide him closely - that Scott stumbled.

The ironic thing about the situation is that, on the surface, in the classroom Scott had not changed. He was not a troublemaker. He did not appear lazy. He "looked" busy. And he WAS busy! But his hard work (or what he perceived as hard work) was getting him nowhere.

Working together, a very understanding and concerned set of parents and a very patient second grade teacher helped him through this period of adjustment. By third grade he appeared to be back on the right track; and aware of his previous year's performance, his third grade teacher took a very personal interest in him. The result was incredible. Scott was a straight- A student all year!

The following September, however, brought a change of school environment. Having advanced to the middle school, Scott found himself (still in the advanced placement program) competing with youngsters from a variety of neighborhoods and in a huge school building with almost 10 times as many students as had been in his friendly, neighborhood elementary school. What's more, the advanced placement teacher with whom he spent most of his day, although she was certainly pleasant and friendly, was also quite businesslike and firm. She expected great things from her students; and she presented many academic challenges - all of which Scott, by all indications (IQ, standardized test scores, etc.) could easily have met.

Mid-way through first quarter, however, it was apparent that something was wrong somewhere. A very frustrated fourth grader brought home a hideous mid-term report. The basic problem is that many assignments were missing; he had simply never turned them in. Follow-up parent-teacher meetings indicated that while Scott was tuned in to the classroom work, when asked to work independently, he appeared to be lost. He didn't know where to begin.

Once again, a very understanding teacher worked closely with Scott's parents, establishing an end-of-the-week system whereby the parents would send in a sheet to be checked, showing how many assignments, if any, were missing. A new notebook check system for Scott himself and more careful supervision of his homework were also employed in an effort to get him back to where he should be. By Christmas of his fourth grade year Scott was once again a productive member of the fourth grade. He still, however, required much overseeing by his parents at home - more than you might expect a 9-year-old would need.

Scott is typical of many **summer children** who lack that extra measure of maturity necessary to develop an independent work attitude. By junior high or high school age many of these youngsters manage to grow up and get their act together; others never do and the syndrome continues on into adulthood.

Whether holding Scott back a year when he was merely five years, six weeks old would have been helpful will never be known. At the time of his kindergarten testing he appeared to be one of the brightest and most outstanding young pupils in the class; and, indeed, he was. Yet he still lacked that additional six months of maturity - something he could NEVER gain on his own. Fortunately, time adds a certain element of growth. But in Scott's case, by the end of the fourth grade year, he had still not caught up with the other members of his advanced placement class.

Aware of this, Scott's parents decided to pull him out of the accelerated academic program with the idea that they would rather have him shine among the average students than falter among the superior ones. The first mid-term report of Scott's fifth grade year showed them they had made the right decision. He was pulling above-average grades (still not as high as what his IQ might indicate he is capable of) but, nonetheless, above average.

What's more, he later admitted to his parents that although he missed some of his friends from the previous year's class, he actually liked school again because he did not feel as pressured. Scott even ran for and won an elected Student Council office during the fifth grade. At the time of this writing, he continues to do well academically - although, his parents report, occasionally a wave of immaturity gets him into some hot water from a disciplinary viewpoint.

The important factor to these parents (as well as to Scott himself) is that the youngster's work is finally getting him somewhere. With much patience and perseverance (on the part of many adults who had a sincere interest in him) he had learned to organize himself a bit better and to work more efficiently. Not all **summer children**, however, are fortunate enough to have such a concerned support group to shelter and to nurture them. They are the ones who continue to merely spin their wheels.

But, hey! Some wheel spinning isn't all bad. We're referring here, literally, to spinning those tiny wheels on Hot Wheels and Matchbox cars or riding a tricycle or even pretending to drive an automobile. In other words, play!

Unfortunately somewhere along the line, the word "play" picked up some rather nasty connotations. Take this letter to syndicated newspaper author John Rosemond:

"I feel you did a great injustice to education. . . Not everyone agrees that. . . a 4-year-old reader will suffer permanent damage to the very nature of intelligence. "The real push for children of kindergarten age to learn to read comes from the fact that first graders are expected to finish a certain standard of accomplishment,

a set of primer books. If a child has done nothing but play for one year in a kindergarten setting, it is a real chore to get all the children learning to read and do math, as expected in grades one, two and three.

"Children love to learn and a 5-year-old can learn to read and enjoy this accomplishment."

This woman's letter is a perfect example of that fascination with teaching preschoolers to read which has permeated much educational thought during the last 25 years or so. Ironically enough, it has also been in this last quarter-century that we have detected what appears to be an epidemic of LD students, a steadily deteriorating reading achievement level, consistently lowered standardized test scores and an odd and unexplained increase in the rate of functional illiteracy among 17-year-olds. Could there be a connection here? You'll get pros and cons on both sides of the question.

The comment we find even more fascinating with this letter, however, is that stabbing reference to children who do "nothing but play" in kindergarten. This points up so clearly the cultural bias that play is a nonproductive activity. And as John Rosemond points out so eloquently in the column in which he responds to this woman's letter, this philosophy is peculiarly American.

"In general," Rosemond writes, "Americans have a habit of judging the merit of things on the basis of product or outcome, and ignoring the process by which the outcome is attained. This is particularly the case when it comes to evaluating things that directly affect our children - things such as television and organized sports and early academics.

"In the latter case," he continues, "it is certainly true that children as young as two can be taught a basic reading vocabulary. The fact that it can be done does not, however, necessarily mean that it should be done."

The parent, psychologist and author Rosemond concludes this particular column with his own astute and simple advice, "I say, 'Just let 'em play.'"

And we say, "Amen!"

Of course, we can probably find many who would beg to differ with us. Many of those parents who are attempting to bring up "Superbaby" are probably choking right about now. But we still stick to our guns and maintain that play, in essence, is a child's "work." It is his means of discovery, of expression, of communication. As stated in the previous chapter, play is an essential element in the growth process.

A German writer, Hildegard Hetzer, puts it much more eloquently and forcefully: **"Many of those adults who are called lazy, or who lack patience, might have gained through play. Only the child who has played long and devotedly grows into a persistent adult who works with joy. If only for this reason we must treat the child who seems too preocupied in his play just as we would treat an adult who carries out his work with diligence and devotion."**

We're delighted when we see or hear anything like this, for it so beautifully supports our own data which suggests that a child does, indeed, have a developmental need to play; and that, in fact, when that kind of playtime is lacking, it shows up later. It's possible, perhaps, that young Scott (who was described earlier in this chapter) simply did not have enough time as a 5-year-old to "just play." He was thrust into a rather demanding kindergarten structure just weeks after his fifth birthday party. It's no wonder that he was later found to be "off-task" in many classroom situations. He may have simply been making up for some lost play time.

This is part of the reason we recommend regular unstructured play time, even for older school-age youngsters. Let them breathe a little after school. Don't push them into homework the moment they come running through the door. Encourage them to let their hair down and fool around a little. There's plenty of time for homework after dinner; and if there isn't, perhaps there should be an investigation into why there are so many after-school assignments.

We're not the only ones who feel this way. In addition to many common-sense parents, there are scores of psychologists and volumes of professional literature which offer virtually the same advice - all in an effort to combat a misconception that our society has picked up somewhere along the line; and that is the absurd notion that play is worthless. For we have come to realize that it is through play that children learn.

Once again we refer to Anne K. Soderman, who so eloquently puts it: "Children at four or five have a genuine need to play and the quality and quantity of the time they spend playing are later seen (or observed to be lacking) in their creative thought, ability to make decisions, and potential for coping with stressful situations."

And what can be more stressful to a kid than failing in school? Yes, failure and lack of play appear to be part of a package. We refer you once again to a quote from Louise Bates Ames. We're repeating it because we feel it sums up much of what our own research proves and we believe:

"Perhaps half of our school failures could be fixed if we started children in school when they're ready. K (kindergarten) requires children to sit quietly, to take turns, to work with workbooks and ditto sheets. But a lot of children at that age need more freedom to move around, to play."

"To sit quietly. . . to work with ditto sheets. . ." If you have an antsy little five-year-old, you might be thinking, "That's just not his bag. He'd rather be home riding his bicycle or playing." And it's true; many youngsters this age might prefer a totally unstructured day to the half-day kindergarten sessions which require more discipline, more self-control and more "work."

Another major element in this picture is the change that occurs as the young child has to adjust to a different adult-child ratio when entering school. Even in preschool/daycare environments, the adult-to-child ratio is usually one to seven or eight; and at home, of course, much lower than that.

Yet, when the child enters the typical kindergarten, he/she must generally cope with a ratio of one to 25 or 30. The reduction in personal attention, emotional support and individual choice can be overwhelming. Under such circumstances the teacher must demand appropriate behavior from all pupils for effective communication (teaching-learning) to take place. This includes seat work, paper-pencil work, quiet work and recitation work.

Curriculum and adult-child ratio, then, often negate the opportunity for learning through play. Yet this type of learning is necessary if later learning through work - so valued in our society - is to be most effective.

Certainly the curriculum includes many messages about work and its important. "But play, too, is important in the child's school day," maintains Nancy King of the University of Maryland. In a recent (Spring, 1986) article in the *Journal of Curriculum and Supervision*, she points out, "Many educators also believe that play is a natural mode of learning for young children."

And those **summer children** who feel behind the eight ball because their classmates are more advanced might also enjoy a good play day away from the school grind now and again, you might reason. It might seem logical, then, that **summer children** would have more of a problem with school attendance than do the older youngsters in the class.

When we began our research project, we were thinking along these same lines; but oddly enough, our look into the attendance aspect has provided some surprising results. Where the girls (in grades one through six) were concerned, there was actually no real difference in the days-absent pattern. The older held back **summer children** boys, however, did show a better attendance record by one day per year than did the **summer children** boys - hardly anything to get too worked up over.

To put it briefly, then, it does not seem evident that any major differences exist between the attendance patterns of **summer children** and held back summer children. It should be noted, though, that the "below seven days absent per year" figure which we found in the Hebron part of our study is quite consistent with the area's above average IQ and achievement test score figures previously noted and cited in the appendix of this book. Perhaps if this study had taken place in a community with a less stable, more mobile complexion, the results would have been different. Right now we can only surmise.

Suffice it to say that while we are pleased that **summer children** are, indeed, out there punching the time clocks in their various schools, and while we are happy that lack of attendance or "playing hooky" doesn't appear to be a major **summer child** syndrome, there are still so many more significant concerns remaining when discussing **summer children**. Is there, for example, too much work and too little play?

Stop and recall. Do you today, as an adult, find yourself using such performance "guides" as the following:

*""I' before 'E' except after 'C'."

83

*"Thirty days hath September, April, June and..."

*"Every Good Boy Does Fine."

If so, you are today using what was learned through play as a tool for adult needs (work). Play does enhance learning. Indeed, it IS learning even in/with "regular" academic content.

True, Saturday's Child "works hard for a living;" and there's certainly nothing wrong with hard work. The American ethic, in fact, has long admired the diligent worker. But when the hours put in do not produce the desired and expected result, when the days are filled with actions that appear to be getting the worker nowhere, when a feeling of failure and incompetence begin to set in, then the worker is in trouble.

Unfortunately, this scenario is so typical of many **summer children** punching the time clock in a "too much, too soon, for too many" environment - those well-meaning, ambitious youngsters who are willing to put in a full day's work and who WOULD reap the fruit of their labor. . . if only they COULD!

Sunday's Child

"Fair and Wise and --"

"Fair and Wise and..."

Being a kid is tough. It always has been. We all had our share of grief and trauma as youngsters, our share of unanswered questions, frustrations and doubts. There were times, to be sure, when it was no picnic being young. But today it's even worse.

We've indicated throughout this book the cultural changes that put so much undue stress and pressure on the 1980s child; and we've also referred you to volumes and volumes on the subject. So there's no sense in being repetitious here.

There is a big point, however, that we'd like to make when talking about Sunday's Child. Surely, we want our kids to be "fair and wise and good and gay" (or, ah, should we say "happy," lest we be misinterpreted!) These are almost every parent's goals; and they have been constant wishes with fathers and mothers of every generation. The difference is that today's children have one big thing working against them - books!

Did you read correctly? Books? Such a statement from a foursome who have worked hard to put THIS book together? That's right! So many kids today are victims of overly-zealous parents who have voraciously devoured almost every book on child rearing to hit the shelves. And, my! How many there are. One trip to a book store or library will get you advice on how to raise your kid's IQ, how to lower his blood pressure, how to teach your baby mathematics, how to make sure your kid can read before he's three, how to have a brighter child, how to have a non-hyperactive child. . . And the list goes on and on and on.

While much of the advice contained in such how-to books is quite sound and even helpful, what we object to is the insinuation that a youngster can be taught anything at any time. Research has proven

86

that this simply is not so. What's more, such ambitious thinking seems to be peculiarly American - at least if we can believe the following story about the famed Swiss philospher Jean Piaget.

It has been written many times that Harvard psychologist Jerome Bruner has stated (and apparently still maintains) that any child can be taught almost any subject at just about any time. The story goes that an American reporter once asked Piaget if he agreed with Bruner's philosophy.

"Only an American would ask," was supposedly Piaget's reply.

Whether there is, indeed, any truth to this vignette is not that important; for it is true that in Europe, the question, "Can you teach any child anything at any time?" is regarded as "the American question."

Yes, we in this land of opportunity do tend to get a bit too ambitious for our own (as well as for our children's) good at times. It's natural. We want all good things for our kids. We want them to be healthier, smarter, richer, better looking than we are or were. And they, no doubt, will be because today's society offers more advantages. When it comes to health consciousness, education, career opportunity and beauty, many things have changed.

But one basic thing has not changed; and that is a child's basic stages of development. No matter how much intellectual stimulation, no matter how many educational toys or devices a youngster has, his basic pattern of development has stayed the same through many generations; and it's likely to remain so.

As a for-instance, in their book, *Don't Push Your Preschooler*, Louise Bates Ames and Joan Ames Chase describe various concepts of time, space, size, shape and number development that occur with youngsters at different levels.

At the age of four, for example, they say that past, present and future words continue to be used freely and about equally. "Many new time words are added here," they say. "The word 'month' comes in; also such broad concepts as 'next summer' and 'last summer.' The child seems to have a reasonably clear understanding of when events of the day take place in relation to each other. He is spontaneously **speedy but slows down if pushed.**" (Our boldface type.)

87

By age five, however, the typical child can usually tell what day it is, name the days of the week in correct order, knows his own age and can project forward and tell how old he will be on his next birthday. Most five-year-olds, too, are interested in clocks - even though most cannot yet tell time; and calendars seem to hold a fascination for them, particularly when discussing birthdays and holidays.

Concerning the sense of space, Ames and Chase say that a typical four-year-old shows much use of expansive words such as "far away," "way up there" and "way off." A new dimension, they point out, is suggested in the use of the term "behind."

At this stage a youngster can generally name his street and city and can, on command, put a ball on, under, in front of, and in back of a chair - all things he could not have done the year before.

By age five, the kindergarten child can usually carry out commands in regard to such terms as "few," "forward," "backward," "tiny," "smooth," and "high," the psychologists note. And by age six his environment has expanded to include relationships between home, neighborhood, school and expanding community. While he is himself the center of his own universe, he begins to show much interest in the sun, moon and planets.

And so a child's development progresses, step by step, stage by stage, in a patterned and orderly fashion according to his or her own individual, internal time clock - influenced, of course, but not totally determined by environmental factors. Just how intelligent a youngster will eventually be also has a lot to do with his genes. Some individuals are simply born with the potential to be smarter than others - just as some individuals' minds are programmed to think differently from others. Have you, for instance, ever known a person who might be termed "shallow" in his thinking or conversation? Beyond topics like the weather, the latest style of clothing, the most popular TV programs (beyond tangibles), he is at a loss for words. No philosophical patter from persons like this.

What we're dealing with here is the difference between concrete and abstract thought. And there's a certain point in the life of a child where he is mature enough to develop some abstract thinking. Up to this point, however, forget it. He must be developmentally ready. Many say that age seven (remember the "age of reason" from your old Catechism lessons?) is generally the level at which a youngster is able to deal with abstract concepts. Then again, some take longer. Some adults, even, never become real abstract thinkers, for not all mind tanks are created equal (much to the chagrin of the mother whose child brings home Cs while the neighbor kid cracks straight As). The point is that not everyone starts out thinking abstractly. We must all arrive at this ability through growth.

It's the same with any human ability or skill; and as you have seen from the few examples of growth patterns at different ages, a mere six months can make a whopping difference. This is, perhaps, especially apparent in dealing with the notions of number and arithmetic. Ames and Chase delineate different abilities at age five years and at age five years, six months (that critical time that we keep talking about so incessantly). From their book:

Five Years: The five-year-old can count thirteen objects with correct pointing. He can count by ones, usually stopping at nineteen or twenty-nine. He can write a few numbers but may not be able to identify what he has written. And he can tell correctly how many fingers he has on one hand.

Five-and-a-Half Years: The child now counts by ones to thirty or more and may count by tens to one hundred and by fives to about fifty. He may be able to write numbers up to twenty but still with some reversals. He can add within ten and subtract within five. He is interested in balanced numbers as two and two, three and three.

Because of this cognitive developmental process and because each individual child's internal time-clock is unique, that six months at the beginning of formal education can be a critical factor in whether or not the youngster begins his schooling experience on a positive or a negative note.

Much of a child's first reaction to the classroom will revolve around a key factor which is totally divorced from academics, and that's his relationship with his peers. When we began our study we unofficially hypothesized that the youngest kids in the class would, most likely, also be the ones to score the lowest in the social relationships category. So we devised a sociometric survey (which is explained in detail in Chapter Four - leadership) and went to work. These questions were given to the pupils in grades one through six:

1. Name three of your good friends in this class.

2. Name three of your classmates with whom you would

like to study.

3. Name three of your classmates with whom you like to play at recess.

4. Name three of your classmates that you want to have on your team in P.E./Gym class.

5. Name three students who need to learn how to share better with others.

Items one, three and five clearly focus on general social relationships. The kids buckled down and answered the questions; and after we tabulated the scores, we found out that on this one we had to eat crow. For the voting results on these three items indicate no strong trend either in favor of or opposed to **summer children.** Contradicting our original hypothesis, the SC boys received 5.4% more votes on the average for being a friend than did the HBSC boys. The SC boys also received 4.88% more votes for playing at recess; and the HBSC unexpectedly received 5.75% more negative votes on the average for sharing better - a category which had been defined for the students as taking turns, not always having to win or be first, etc.

The girls also had mixed results on these three items. The sharing better results (see table in appendix) support the hypothesis with the held back summer girls receiving 6.60% FEWER average votes per child than did the summer girls -- the exact opposite pattern as for the boys. The friends item found another draw with no major difference in results; but the play at recess votes again favored the older held back summer girls by 3.92%

So you see, our original hypothesis received a slightly rejecting score in general. But when broken down into male and female categories, an interesting trend emerges. For the fellows, our idea was totally rejected; but for the gals it was accepted.

Question number two on study helpers brought even more surprises. This item was designed to focus on the children's perceptions of who were good students and might be able to help the voter as he or she studied new material. The query was defined orally as "persons who could help you learn better." Once again the results shot down our preconceived notions. For (see table in appendix) there was no major difference between **summer children** and held back **summer children** for the boys. The summer girls, however, unexpectedly received 6.04% more votes on the average than did the held back summer girls, thus AGAIN rejecting our hypothesis. This interesting tally could be partially explained by the fact that the summer girls were found to have an average IQ score 15 points higher than the held back summer girls (115 vs. 100) while for boys the SC had only a 7 point (107 vs. 100) advantage.

The last category for which the students' perceptions of their classmates was sought focused on athletic and physical abilities; and once again we received mixed results. The children were asked to select three classmates to be on their own team in a gym class. These three were to be chosen because they would give the team a good chance to win the race, the game, the event, etc.

The results (see table in appendix) show that once again the summer boys received an average of 5.04% MORE votes than did the held back summer boys - again, contrary to what we would have predicted. The summer girls, however, turned in results which WERE consistent with our expectations, as they received 4.14% more votes per child than did the younger summer girls.

Overall, then, our numbers present a very mixed picture when it comes to **summer children** and social relationships. When we subdivide into boys and girls, though, rejection of our hypothesis (boys) and acceptance (girls) is more clearly evident. Our expectation that the older students (the held back **summer children**) would receive a greater percent-per-child of the maximum votes possible than did the younger **summer children** was tested seven times for both males and females. (The leadership questions discussed earlier were also used at this time.) The results for the boys, as you have seen, soundly rejected our predictions on five items. We also had a modest rejection on one item and a draw on another. The results for the girls, on the other hand, were rather different. The older girls were "winners" on four items, "losers" on one item and even on two items.

Although not directly related to the major questions involved in our extended study, the different vote results between the two sexes is most revealing. In general, the girls were much more willing to select boys than boys were to select girls. The results for all boys and all girls (see table in appendix) indicates the average percent-of-maximum vote possible received by each boy and each girl.

Overall, the young ladies "won" as choices for study companion and for being in charge of the room if the teacher were to be gone - both positive choices. The boys, however, "won" on only one item - being on "my" PE team; and they were also big "winners" on both negative items - needing to behave better and to share better.

These results tend to support the old theory that schooling is geared more closely to the stereotype of feminine characteristics. They also support the fact that girls tend to mature faster than boys of the same age. This last point may also explain, in part, why there were unexpected results for the boys when **summer children** and held back **summer children** students were compared.

But while these sociometric data results turned in a mixed bag of results, other data obtained in our total studies were quite clear-cut, as you have seen. To recap, it was found that:

* **75% of all the students in the study who had failed at least one year of school were, indeed, summer children; and two-thirds of these failures were boys.**

* **Summer children girls were off-task during class nearly three times as much as held back summer children girls; summer boys were off-task nearly twice as much as their older, held back classmates.**

* **In spite of their IQ score disadvantages, the held back summer girls OUTSCORED the summer children on the Iowa Basic Skills; and the held back summer boys scored within one percentile point, thus indicating that greater maturity may enable one to use what intelligence he/she has much more efficiently and effectively.**

We want to help you make the major decision as to whether or not to have a child wait a year before starting school or moving on to first grade. Consider this to be a "summer storm." Storm signals will give you clues as to what to expect.

The first dark cloud - chronological age at the time of school entrance - is a major signal. Following the next paragraph is a listing of other "clouds" to look for. The more clouds you find, the larger the approaching storm is likely to be.

To put it succinctly, our total studies indicate just what we had hypothesized at the beginning of our project - that if you have a summer child, then you should seriously consider holding him back.

92

Notice we use the term "consider." Realizing that each case is individual, but also stressing the fact that we feel MOST youngsters would benefit by waiting until age five years, six months to enter kindergarten, we've come up with some criteria to consider before making a decision. If you are faced with this crucial question of whether or not to enroll your less than five- year-old, six-month child in kindergarten, stop and consider him or her in light of the following characteristics:

•**Attention span. Can your five-year-old stay with a task, game or book for 15 to 20 minutes at a time?**

•**Emotional level. Does your son or daughter cry when left alone? Is he or she easily frightened?**

•**Small muscle skills. How well does your child handle eating utensils? Crayon? Scissors?**

•**Large muscle skills. How well does your child ride a bike? Go up and down steps? Walk and/or run without falling?**

•**Social skills. Can your youngster interact peacefully with other children?**

•**Memory level. Does your summer child know his or her address? Remember past special events? Recall the words to prayers or songs?**

•**General health. Must your child go often to the doctor, other than for general checkups, thus missing school?**

•**Chronological age. Was your youngster premature? Does he prefer younger children for playmates?**

•**Sex. Boys tend to be less mature than girls; but even girls can benefit greatly from added maturity.**

•**Speech clarity. Speech problems are often forecasters of later reading problems.**

•**Reading interest. Does your child show a strong interest in being read to at home?**

•Community pattern. If it is common to hold back children, a child who starts kindergarten at four years, 11 months may well have classmates age six years or older!

•Birth weight. Was the child of average or above weight (given family background)?

•Length and/or difficulty of labor. These tend to be associated with later school and learning problems.

•Composition of family. One, two or more parents, adults? Supportive? Abusive?

•Birth order. First, middle, last? Also, age differences between siblings.

•Stability of family. Continuity of relationships?

These are some of the basic areas we feel you should consider before talking with counselors and teachers and arriving at a decision - one which, of course, should be based on the individual personality, characteristics and needs of that very special and very unique child who has been entrusted to your care.

We've gone on and on about **summer children** who WOULD succeed in school. . . if only they COULD. Well, maybe these youngsters COULD succeed, COULD get started on the road to education with a more positive self-esteem, if more parents, administrators, teachers and counselors WOULD consider some of the ideas we've researched and discussed. We're not presenting our CAUTION statement as a cure-all or panacea for school failures and/or for kids who feel rotten about themselves. But it COULD be a beginning. It COULD rescue **summer children** from the "too much, too soon, for too many" cycle and put them on a more positive road to personal satisfaction and fulfillment. It COULD help make Sunday's Child - and EVERY child - just the type of youngster every parent desires: ". . . fair and wise and good and gay."

But even more significantly, it COULD make a world of difference in the life of the most important summer child in the world - YOURS!

Questions and Answers

Over the past several years we have spoken to dozens of groups of educators and/or parents and have received hundreds of letters and phone calls as a result of wire service news articles and our publications in various professional journals.

We have found the same basic questions to be raised over and over. While our answers are contained within this book, we feel that the following brief, but direct, summary will be of value to our readers.

Q. Because there will nearly always be at least a 12-month span between the oldest and youngest children in a grade, won't delaying the entry of summer children merely shift the "burden" of being youngest to the 'spring children,' etc.?

A. If one measures success using the old normal curve, then by definition there will always be winners and losers; and the "new" youngest group is most likely to be well represented in the latter group.

However, this ignores the fact that as the entire class gains in developmental readiness and maturity, all will be better able to cope and learn. The class's average scores will increaase and fewer children will need special help or remediation. In short, the gap between highs and lows has been found to narrow when the total group is more ready for school.

As more children are seen by their peers as being "OK," social acceptance and shared leadership is found to be more widespread within the group.

Q. My summer child is very bright. I'm afraid he/she will

be bored even next year. If we delay entry, won't the problem of boredom be even worse next year?

A. We contend that brightness is not the real issue. The "degree" of being brighter than his/her peers will only change slightly over that one-year span of time. If the school provides for such individual differences with alternative assignments, enrichment, etc., then no problem would exist in either case.

If the school does not do this and boredom is a factor, we believe the evidence clearly indicates that the older, more mature and developmentally ready child is much better able to provide self-motivation, self-stimulation, and self-control. Very bright, but very young, children were found to be among the most off-task/inattentive of all the pupils and tended to be underachievers - as a result developing very poor study habits which tend to be long lasting.

Q. My summer child is already physically large for his/her age group. Won't delaying school entrance or repeating an early grade make this "problem" much worse?

A. As in the previous question, physical size is not the real issue since the child will only change his/her relative position within the group very slightly. If in the top 15% now, delaying or repeating may only move the child to the top eight to 10% - a rather small change.

The key question is whether or not the child is to be a big follower or a big leader. The data clearly indicate that the youngest children are far less likely to develop leadership skills/traits than are the oldest ones. Will Johnnie's "bigness" be used in productive and positive ways by him or become used by others for their own purposes?

Incidentally, with the increase in the number of sports opportunities for girls and greater variety of sports for boys as well, some parents have chosen (rightly or wrongly) to "redshirt" their youngster for this athletic reason alone.

Q. Is a delayed start or early grade repeat a guarantee of later success or prevention of problems?

A. In a word, "No!"

What we have said in the narrative you have just read and what is in the data presented in the appendix which follows clearly indicate that no such promises can be made. The chances, however, of such a more developmentally ready child having success in school are much higher than for the less ready child who may even be brighter.

The odds for success clearly favor the older child because fewer potential "storm clouds" (see chapter seven) are in the sky (life) of these youngsters. It is still possible for there to be some rain, but much less likely.

Q. Delaying the start of school for boys is understandable, but why do you suggest this just as much for girls?

A. Physiologically, girls start life with about a one-month advantage over boys. By ages five to six, the girls are nearly six months ahead developmentally and by ages 11 and 12, they are about two years ahead. Girls are also typically much healthier.

A number of educators contend that we should not start formal reading instruction until age seven; and math, until age eight. Scandanavian countries start youngsters in first grade at age seven, unlike the United States where age six is the norm. The Scandanavian pupils learn to read and write and compute - in several languages - with great success; and experience fewer failures than found in the United States. (Age, while very important, is not the only reason for this.)

Thus if girls are "held back" from starting school, they are even more ready for what's expected and their odds for success are even higher than for the same age boys who delayed their start also.

Q. Why don't the states change their laws for "age-at-school-entrance-dates"?

A. They have!

At least many have done this. Within the past 10 years nearly half of the states have moved their "starting date" from the months of November and December to a date in September. Missouri has recently passed a law to move its date to July 1st by 1988 - the earliest in the nation at this writing. It passed the legislature on the first effort. Such was not the case in Illinois where it took many years to pass a 1985 law which will move its December date to September.

Traditions are usually hard to break; but the evidence now available is helping more and more states to make such changes. We hope this book will help bring more such changes as the "show me" state has "shown us!"

If "saving" kids from problems will not motivate legislators, then perhaps the real possibility of saving money otherwise needed for special classes, repeating of a grade (an extra year of per-pupil aid) and special equipment will convince them.

Q. If a child needs to repeat a grade for academic, social, emotional and/or physical reasons, when should the repeat be done?

A. Although this is an entirely separate area of study from ours, what we have read strongly suggests that the earlier a repeat takes place, the more likely it is to have positive results. The best place to repeat is at home or in a good pre-school or nursery school before starting kindergarten.

Some school districts have accommodated this need by designing a special pre-kindergarten class and curriculum for age-ready but developmentally unready children.

Other districts have created a special class with such titles as "junior first grade," "transitional first grade" and "pre-first grade." The bottom line is that all such programs are designed to reduce the emotional trauma of too much, too soon, for too many by increasing the odds of success for these children. Thus school/learning/education will be more likely to have a positive emotional association for them for the rest of their lives.

Q. My summer child did quite well in the early grades, but seems to have hit a real snag in third and fourth grades. Why?

A. It is not at all unusual for this to occur. The child from a verbal family may do well in the early years; but as the learning expectations become more complex and broaden to include more abstract and less concrete skills, materials, etc., problems develop.

100

The age of group skills (Cub Scouts, Brownies, Little League, etc.) calls for new abilities which some of the summer children have not yet developed.

Being able to share, to deal with win/lose situations, to work cooperatively, to be self-controlled and to be physically adept is more important at this age. Self-confidence is related to self-image. If peers are rejecting or finding fault or teasing, then self-concept is reduced and a downward spiral becomes very common.

Q. Should parents or schools make the decisions to delay a child's school entry or to repeat a grade based upon the chronological age factor alone?

A. No!

We strongly believe in a thorough multi-faceted assessment process. As discussed in the section on "storm clouds" in the final chapter, we believe that there are many factors to be considered.

The more of those factors found to be related to a particular child, the greater the risk for that child if school entrance is not delayed or a grade repeated as early as possible. The age factor is a major one and thus may cause the home and/or school to give attention to the situation.

A few children who are more than five years, six months of age at school entrance will be found to be unready. A few who are very young will be found to be quite ready. In general, however, the odds are very strong in favor of delayed entry.

Appendix

Appendix
Ames & Ilg

"Your Six Year Old Loving and Defiant"

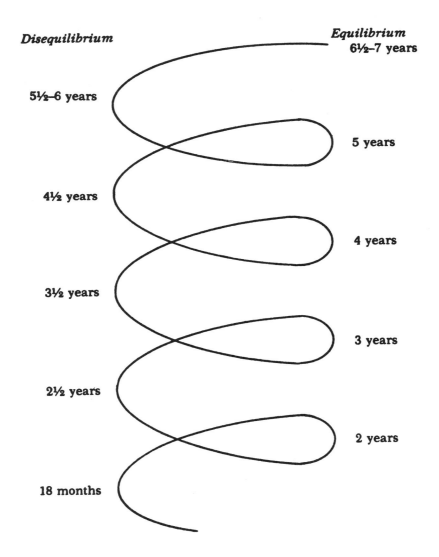

Disequilibrium

Equilibrium
6½–7 years

5½–6 years

5 years

4½ years

4 years

3½ years

3 years

2½ years

2 years

18 months

Appendix

Gilmore - Wapakoneta, Ohio

PERCENT SC AND HBSC WITH ABOVE AVERAGE, AND BELOW AVERAGE

GRADE LEVEL EQUIVALENT SCORES ON THE IOWA TEST OF BASIC SKILLS

Grade-level Equivalent Score Levels	BOYS		GIRLS		TOTAL	
	SC	HBSC	SC	HBSC	SC	HBSC
Above Average	26.67%	79.17%	22.22%	71.43%	24.24%	77.42%
Average	33.33%	8.33%	50.00%	28.57%	42.42%	12.90%
Below Average	40.00%	12.50%	27.78%	----	33.33%	9.68%

Gilmore

PERCENT SC AND HBSC RECEIVING ABOVE AVERAGE, AND BELOW
AVERAGE CUMULATIVE TEACHER ASSIGNED GRADES

Level of Teacher-Given Grades	BOYS		GIRLS		TOTAL	
	SC	HBSC	SC	HBSC	SC	HBSC
Above Average	46.67%	80.77%	60%	100%	54.29%	85.71%
Average	26.67%	11.54%	30%	----	28.57%	8.57%
Below Average	26.67%	7.69%	10%	----	17.14%	5.71%

Gilmore

APPENDIX
Steven R. Huff - Beavercreek, OH , Study

SUBJECTS	Starters	Delayed Starters
Number of boys	15	9
Number of girls	6	6
Mean age to begin school	5 yr. 4 mo.	6 yr. 1 mo.
Mean age at time of testing	8 yr. 2 mo.	8 yr. 2 mo.
Mean years spent in school at time of testing	2 yr. 7 mo.	2 yr. 1 mo.

Early Starters

Reading___ 2.3 Read like children who had been in the second grade for 3 months.

Math_____ 1.9 Performed math like children who had been in the first grade for 9 months.

Total Test 2.1 = 1 month in the second grade

Early starters had been in school 24.4 months at the time of testing.

Delayed Starters

Reading_____ 2.8 = 8 months in the second grade.

Math_____ 2.2 = 2 months in the second grade.

Total Test 2.6 = 6 months in the second grade.

Delayed starters had been in school 18.0 months at the time of testing.

The "Early Starters" scored fairly well but those who waited an extra year scored about one-half year higher. What is even more significant is that it took "early starters" as a group more than six extra months of schooling to achieve their results. Out of the 21 students who started kindergarten, 15 were retained in grade one or two. No "delayed starters" were retained in their first two years of school.

APPENDIX
Swartz, et al

Table 2*

Subject Grouping by School Entrance Age

Birthdates	Learning Disabled	Standard Program
December–February (5-8 to 5-6) (yrs – months)	8	7
March – May (5-5 to 5-3)	5	17
June–August (5-2 to 5-0)	12	16
September–November (4-9 to 4-11)	20	10

*from : Stanley L. Swartz, et al, "Incidence of Learning Disabilities and Early School Entrance," Illinois School Research and Development. Vol. 20, No. 3, Spring, 1984, p.26.

Note : Illinois has had an entrace age cutoff date of December 1st. By 1988 this will become September 1st due in part to research findings such as these by Dr. Swartz and his Western Illinois University Colleagues.

Troy Advanced Junior Level English

ADVANCED JUNIOR LEVEL ENGLISH NINE WEEK TERM
PAPER "A" GRADES 1983-1984 BY CHRONOLOGICAL AGE AT
SCHOOL ENTRANCE (34 STUDENTS)

AGE AT SCHOOL ENTRANCE	NUMBER OF "A's"	% OF "A's"
OLDEST 20% (7=N)	5	71.4%
YOUNGEST 20% (7-N)	1	14.3%

107

Appendix
Uphoff - Hebron, Nebraska

<u>MEAN % OF TIME OFF-TASK BY GROUPS OF STUDENTS</u>

GIRLS			BOYS		
SC	HBSC	ALL OTHER	SC	HBSC	ALL OTHER
7.05	2.04	4.44	7.25	4.21	6.06

−Uphoff

<u>OFF TASK RANK ORDER FOR SC AND HBSC</u>

CATEGORY	GIRLS	BOYS	TOTAL
A. % Summer Children rank ordered in the **upper** third (**most off task**)	41.03%	45.83%	42.85%
B. % Heldback SC rank ordered in the **upper** third (**most** off task)	11.11%	23.50%	19.2%
C. % SC rank ordered in the lowest third (**least** off task)	25.64%	25.00%	25.40%
D. %HBSC rank ordered in the lowest third (**least** off task)	44.40%	35.30%	38.50%

−Uphoff

Appendix
Uphoff - Hebron, Nebraska

SUMMARY OF AVERAGE I.Q. SCORE* BY GROUPS FOR GRADES 1-6

GIRLS				BOYS			
SC	HBSC	OTHER GIRLS	ALL GIRLS	SC	HBSC	OTHER BOYS	ALL BOYS
115.39	100.75	109.58	111.42	106.98	99.81	108.93	107.53
FOR FIRST GRADERS ONLY							
122.50	107.00	113.91	116.39	118.88	106.4	116.25	114.40

-Uphoff

*Scores used came from a variety of tests given by different schools and at
different times by Hebron officials. Some scores were as much as "three
years old" at the time of use (April 1982).

CUMULATIVE PERCENTILE SCORE AVERAGES FOR IOWA TEST OF BASIC SKILLS TAKEN APRIL 1982 GRADES 1-6

GIRLS				BOYS			
SC	HBSC	OTHER GIRLS	ALL GIRLS	SC	HBSC	OTHER BOYS	ALL BOYS
69.29	71.6	70.63	70.17	62.10	61.85	65.28	64.24
FOR FIRST GRADERS							
78.33	88.0	68.73	73.61	62.25	71.20	57.42	61.62

-Uphoff

Appendix
Uphoff - Hebron, Nebraska - Sociometric Survey

Average Percent-of-Maximum Vote Per Child by Groups on Social Relationship Items

ITEM	BOYS			GIRLS		
	SC	HBSC	OTHERS	SC	HBSC	OTHERS
1. Friends (+)	18.10%	12.70%	13.60%	13.76%	13.27%	15.38%
2. Play (+)	15.21%	10.33%	14.80%	14.52%	18.44%	14.56%
3. Share Better (-)	16.03%	21.78%	16.04%	11.65%	5.05%	11.62%

Average Percent-of-Maximum Vote Per Child by Groups on
Helps-Me-Study-Well Item

BOYS			GIRLS		
SC	HBSC	Others	SC	HBSC	Others
11.52%	11.32%	14.74%	16.42%	10.38%	15.16%

Average Percent-of-Maximum Vote Per Child by Groups on
Leadership-Responsibility Items

ITEM	BOYS			GIRLS		
	SC	HBSC	OTHERS	SC	HBSC	OTHERS
4. Behave better (-)	16.47%	24.23%	22.79%	6.62%	2.11%	4.77%
5. Be in charge (+)	10.80%	8.58%	10.17%	18.73%	18.16%	19.94%

Average Percent-of-Maximum Vote Per Child by Groups on
Physical-Athletic Skills

BOYS			GIRLS		
SC	HBSC	Others	SC	HBSC	Others
21.22%	16.18%	21.03%	7.02%	11.16%	7.08%

Bibliography

Ames and Ilg, *Your Six Year Old Loving and Defiant*, Delta Books, 1979, Dell Publishing Co.

Ames, Louise Bates, Ph.D., and Chase, Joan Ames, Ph.D. *Don't Push Your Preschooler*. New York: Harper and Row, 1980.

Ames, Louise Bates, Ph.D. *Is Your Child in the Wrong Grade?* Lumberville, Pa.: Modern Learning Press, 1978.

Ames, Louise Bates, Ph.D., and Ilg, Frances L. *Your Five Year Old: Sunny and Serene*. New York: Delacorte, 1976

Bowen, Ezra, Trying to Jump-Start Toddlers, *TIME*, April 7, 1986, pg. 66.

Bridgman, Anne, "Preschool Pressure, Later Difficulties Linked in Study," *Education Week*, April 23, 1986

Briggs, Dorothy C. *Your Child's Self Esteem*. Garden City, New York: Doubleday and Co., Inc., Dolphin Books, 1970, 1975

Caplan, Theresa and Frank. *The Early Childhood Years*. The Princeton Center for Infancy and Early Childhood, New York: Bantam Books, 1983.

Christensen, Kim, "More young feel despair, kill selves," *Dayton Daily News*, May 7, 1984, pg. 3.

Diamond, Grace, "The Birthdate Effect - A Maturational Effect?" *Journal of Learning Disabilities*, March, 1983, pp. 161-164..

DiPasquale, Glenn W., Ph.D.; Moule, Allan D., Ph.D., and Flewelling, Robert W., Ph.D., "The Birthdate Effect," *Journal of Learning Disabilities*, May, 1980.

111

Dreikurs, Rudolf. *Children: The Challenge.* New York: Hawthorn/-Dutton, 1964

Elkind, David, *The Hurried Child.* Reading, Mass.: Addison-Wesley Publishing Co., 1981.

Elkind, David, "The Miseducation of Young Children," *Phi Delta Kappan*, May, 1986, pp. 631-636.

Forester, John J., "At What Age Should Children Start School?" *School Executive*, Vol. 74, March, 1953, pp. 80-81.

Gott, Margaret E., "The Effect of Age Difference at Kindergarten Entrance on Achievement and Adjustment in Elementary School," University of Colorado dissertation, 1963.

Hall, E. Vance, "Does Entrance Age Affect Achievement?" *The Elementary School Journal,* April, 1963, pp. 391-396.

Hamalainen, Arthur, "Kindergarten - Primary Entrance Age in Relation to Later School Adjustment, " *The Elementary School Journal*, March, 1952.

Hedges, William D., *At What Age Should Children Enter First Grade - A Comprehensive Review of the Research*, University Microfilms, 1977.

Hildegrand, John, "Flunking Kindergarten Tends to Set Some Parents Back," *The Cincinnati Enquirer*, (copyright, Newsday Syndicate), September 12, 1983.

Huff, Steven R., Beavercreek, Ohio Study, 1983-1984.

Ilg, Frances L., Ph.D., and Ames, Louise Bates., Ph.D. *Child Behavior from Birth to Ten.* New York: Harper and Row Publishers, 1955.

Kaercher, Dan, "When It's Smart for a Youngster to Repeat a Grade," *Better Homes and Gardens*, June, 1984, pp. 21-23

Kemme, Steve, "Gifted Child - Accelerated Learning Harmful, Educator Says," *The Cincinnati Enquirer*, May 5, 1984.

King, Inez, "Effect of Age Entrance into Grade I Upon Achievement in Elementary School," *The Elementary School Journal*, February,

1955, pp. 331-336.

King, Nancy, "When Educators Study Play in Schools," *Journal of Curriculum and Supervision*, Spring, 1986, pp. 233-246.

Knechtly, Patricia, "Does Early Entrance into School Affect the Reading Achievement of Early Entrants?' an unpublished research paper, Wright State University, Dayton, Ohio, May, 1980.

Matheny, Ruth A., "Coming, Ready or Not?" *Today's Catholic Teacher*, December, 1984, pg. 50.

Lacayo, Richard (with Jeanne-Marie North and other bureaus). "Getting Off to a Quick Start," TIME, October 8, 1984, pg. 62.

McDaniel, Joyce, Englewood Elementary School Study; Northmont, Ohio, 1983-1984, an unpublished research paper, Wright State University, Dayton, OH, May 1984.

Mawhinney, Paul E., "We Gave Up on Early Entrance," *The Michigan Education Journal*, May, 1964.

May, Deborah C., Ed.D., and Welch, Edward, Ph.D., "Developmental Placement: Does It Prevent Future Learning?' *Journal of Learning Disabilities*, June-July, 1984.

Miller, Vera, "Academic Achievement and Social Adjustment of Children Young for their Grade Placement," *The Elementary School Journal*, February, 1957, pp. 257-263.

Moore, Raymond S., and Dorothy N., Better Late Than Early. New York: *Reader's Digest Press*, 1977.

Rosemond, John, "Parents," *Dayton Daily News*, (syndicated column), June 3, 1983, pg. 30.

Roberts, Debbie, "School Districts Set Up Transitional First Grades," *Deerfield Review*, March 31, 1983.

Soderman, Anne T., "Schooling All 4-Year-Olds: An Idea Full of Promise, Fraught With Pitfalls," *Education Week*, March 14, 1984, pg. 19.

Swartz, Dr. Stanley L., and Back, Dr. Donald H., "School Entrance Age and Problems in Learning: A Proposal for Change," *Illinois Principal*, September, 1981, pp. 10-11.C

Swartz, Dr. Stanley L.; Joy, Kathryn; and Block, Gail, "Incidence of Learning Disabilities and Early School Entrance," *Illinois School Research and Development*, Spring, 1984, pp. 23-28.

Uphoff, James K., "Sociometric Survey Used to Study Problems of Summer Children," *The Review,* Ohio Council for Social Studies, Vol. 20, N0. 1, Spring, 1984, pp. 33-36.

Uphoff, James K., and Gilmore, June E., "Pupil Age at School Entrance - How Many are Ready for Success?" *Educational Leadership*, September, 1985, pp. 86-90.

Weaver, Peg, "Teen Suicide," *The Lutheran*, June 6, 1984, pp. 5-6.

_____ , "A Nation at Risk," *The Chronicle of Higher Education*, May 4, 1983.

_____ , "Bringing Up Superbaby," (Copyright *Newsweek*, Inc., All rights reserved. Reprinted by permission) March 28, 1983, pp. 62-68.

_____ , "Children Starting Kindergarten Early Are More Likely to Fail at School," *The National Enquirer*, October 13, 1985.

_____ , "Criteria for Selecting Play Equipment for Early Childhood Education," a pamphlet by Community Playthings, Rifton, New York, 1982.

_____ , "Homework at an Early Age," (Copyright *Newsweek*, Inc., All rights reserved. Reprinted by permission) April 21, 1986. pg. 75.

_____ , "Readers' Views," *The Cincinnati Enquirer*, September 22, 1983.

_____ , "Teen Suicide: Seeing No One to Help," *Dayton Daily News*, May 26, 1984, pg. 2.

_____ , "Why reading aloud makes learning fun," *U.S. News and World Report*, March 17, 1986, pp. 65-66.